The Independent Bookworm

ABOUT THE BOOK

Once upon a time in a world where magic and technology collide with unexpected consequences…

Ember Ash toils in the family's clockwork shop under her stepfather's watchful eye and dreams of magic. When she buys a fairy in a cage, her life takes a turn for the weird even though the fairy's magic is but weak. Can Ember outwit her jealous stepsister and find a magic of her own?

What if the Brother's Grimm hadn't realized how capable „Cinderella" really was?

ABOUT THE AUTHOR

Ever since she was born, Katharina Gerlach had her head in the clouds. She and her three younger brothers grew up in the middle of a forest in the heart of the Luneburgian Heather. After romping through the forest with imagination as her guide, the tomboy learned to read and disappeared into magical adventures, past times or eerie fairytale woods.

She never returned to Earth for long, although she managed to successfully finish training as a landscape gardener, study forestry and gain a PhD. But then, she discovered her vocation: storytelling and realized she'd have to write to make her dream of sharing her stories with others come true.

Katharina loves to write Fantasy, Science Fiction and Historical Novels for all age groups. At present, she is writing at her next project in a small house near Hildesheim, Germany, where she lives with her husband, three children and a dog.

Mehr Informationen: http://de.KatharinaGerlach.com

EMBER ASH
CINDERELLA
TREASURES RETOLD 9

Katharina Gerlach

Ember Ash, Treasures Retold 9
published by the Independent Bookworm, USA und D
This book is also available as eBook. It has been published in English and in German.

If you find any typos or formatting problems in this eBook, please contact the publisher (www.IndependentBookworm.de).
All rights reserved. This book may not be reproduced, distributed, transmitted, or stored in whole or in part by any means, including graphics and illustrations, without the express written permission of the publisher or the author. You may use short citations for reviews.
This is a work of fiction. The characters, events, and locations portrayed in this book are fictitious. Any similarity or resemblance to actual events, locales or persons, living or dead, is entirely coincidental and not intended by the author.

© 2016, all rights remain with the author
© 2017, cover art by Katharina Kolata
© 2017, title background by Corona Zschusschen
© 2014, logo by colorgraphix
© 2017, paragraph divider by Katharina Kolata
editor: Ethan James Clarke
printed On-Demand Publishing LLC, 100 Enterprise Way, Suite A200, Scotts Valley, CA 95066, USA, www.createspace.com

ISBN-13 978-3-95681-101-2

More Information can be found on the publisher's website:
http://www.IndependentBookworm.de

For my family. I couldn't have done it without you.

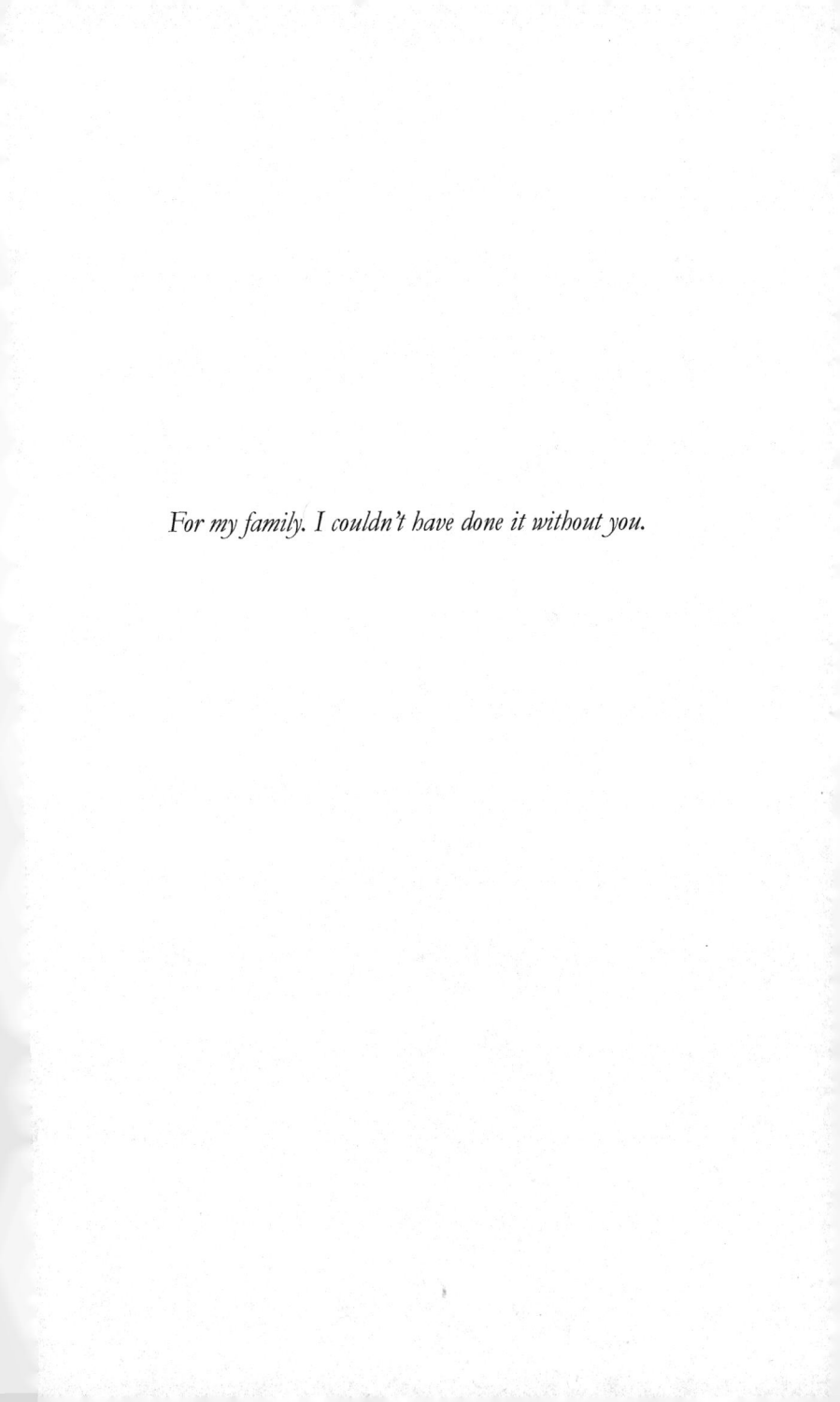

Table of Contents

Ember Ash 9
Bonus: The Goat's Curse 53
The Original: Cinderella 95
More Books in the Series 106

Ember Ash

Very carefully, Ember smoothed out the crinkles in the leaf gilding. Her tongue inadvertently followed the movement of her brush. This was her last leaf of gold, and the customer would come to pick up his clockwork coach any time. Making a mistake wouldn't do.

"Ember, where's the silver wire?" Her stepfather poked his head through the curtain of her work cubicle. "I can't find it anywhere."

"It should be in the top drawer of the supply cabinet."

"Don't you think I looked there?" He pushed his fat belly through the narrow passage. "Lilly and Rose haven't got any."

"I'm not working with silver at the moment." She pointed to the nearly finished clockwork coach, thinking it wise not to tell her stepfather how often Rose had sold silver wire to the goldsmith next door so she could buy herself another dress or yet another pair of shoes. On her left cheek, she still felt the slap from last week when she had told him Rose was only pretending to be working.

"I really, really wish I had a son." Sighing, her stepfather turned and squeezed through the narrow opening again. With regret, Ember heard one of his shirt buttons pop. *That means sewing tonight.*

She laid the brush aside and examined her work. The coach seemed magical. It looked as if she'd made it out of a real pumpkin; she matched the color that well. And the golden manes of the horses sparkled in the dim light of the plain bulb over her workbench. All she needed to do now was attach the horses to the pumpkin carriage and she'd be done.

"Ember! Get your ass out here." Her stepfather's voice carried over his shoulder, and Ember jumped. She hadn't realized that him coming here was his way of fetching her. In a hurry, she put the empty gold box down and ran after him into the main workroom.

"Get three talers worth of silver wire. Tell Geoffrey to put it on my list. I'll settle the list after the weekend."

Before Ember could acknowledge the order, Rose rushed in from the shop. "But Father! You don't really want to send *her* for something so important, do you?"

"Why not, Precious?" He smiled at his daughter. "Lilly is at her friend's today, and seeing that you're busy with the shop…"

"I guess she could take my place for a while." Rose looked Ember over. Ember rubbed a spec of gold stuck to the back of her hand, embarrassingly aware of the fact that her plain work clothes paled in comparison to Rose's carefully tailored dress. Rose shrugged. "She will do. At least she's not dirty this time."

"You really want to walk through half the town to get me my silver?" Her father beamed as if she'd made him a present.

"You know how much I adore Geoffrey." Rose pushed Ember to the opening leading into the shop.

Happy to get out of the way, Ember obeyed. She hadn't been to the shop often, and when she had, it had always been night, so she looked around wide-eyed. Clowns grinned down from shelves ready to shake their heads or sing a song at the turn of a crank. Ballerinas stood on boxes waiting for their time to dance. Balls with bells inside, hoops and rings, colorful paper mannequins, porcelain dolls – every available surface was covered with the things they sold, and she'd made most of them. Lilly and Rose had no talent for mechanics, and her stepfather didn't do more than what was absolutely necessary to keep the shop stocked. *So many wonderful toys ... it's a kid's paradise, full of potential for imagination and magic.* The voices behind her grew quiet, which meant that Rose had finally left. Ember stood straighter, feeling like the shop owner for a moment. A smile spread over her face.

The bell rang, and a young man strode in. A shock of brown, hard-to-smooth hair fell into his face, obscuring his eyes. His wide shoulders and slender hips stretched the fabric of the exquisitely tailored outfit he wore, as if he'd outgrown it a little while ago. He clearly was no simple servant; maybe a second son of a not-too-well-off lesser noble.

Ember's smile faltered for a second, then she caught herself. "How can I serve you, sir?"

"Oh, uhm..." The young man seemed to feel as uncomfortable as she did, so she smiled some more.

He cleared his throat. "I... I mean, a friend of mine asked me to pick up a toy chariot he'd ordered."

"Are you talking about the order from the palace? In that case I'll need proof that you're indeed allowed to pick it up." Ember cocked her head a little, hoping it looked apologetic. "Orders by the palace's administration."

"Sure, sure. No problem." The young man rummaged through his pockets. "Would I... I mean... Are you going to pack it? I'd so much like to see it."

Ember understood his curiosity. If she were sent to pick up a gift like that, she'd feel the same. "I can bring it through to the shop so you can look at it while I pack it."

"That'd be splendid. Meanwhile I'll find that certificate for you."

Ember hurried through the workroom, past her stepfather who sat snoring in his seat, into her own workroom. Gently she picked up her work and hurried back to the shop.

"Wow!" The young man's jaw dropped when she put horse and carriage down and connected them. A pleasurable shiver ran through Ember. "It can move, too." She toggled the tiny lever on the drawbar, and the horses began to walk, pulling the carriage along.

"Incredible. Did you use magic?" The stranger's face was hopeful.

Ember laughed. She knew the answer to that. "Naturally not. There's no such thing as magic anymore."

"Well…" The young man bent forward until his face nearly touched hers. Ember's heart raced. She held her breath. When he whispered, his fringe tickled her cheek, causing eddies of excitement throughout her body. "I wouldn't be too sure about that. I've heard rumors that there are pockets of magic left up north."

"Really?" Ember pretended not to be interested. Confessing to be interested in magic could be dangerous. Most people these days were afraid of the unknown force. Also, she still struggled to get control over the strange, new feelings this… this boy woke in her.

"A merchant from Bergia told the younger prince recently that he'd seen a unicorn in the forest."

"A unicorn…" Try as she might, Ember couldn't keep the awe from her voice. "I'd love to see it with my own two eyes."

"Me too. And I will. You'll see." The stranger straightened. "Careful! The chariot."

Just before the first pair of horses reached the edge of the table, Ember stopped the mechanism. Silently she wrapped first the animals then the carriage in thin paper and placed everything in a cardboard box. The whole time she felt the stranger's gaze burn on her skin. She found it harder and harder to breathe normally.

When she finished packing the little toy, she asked for the palace's certificate. It was ornately decorated but didn't give a name. What a pity. The sigil was genuine though, so she held out the box with the toy to the young man, her gaze met his.

He blushed. "You're quite… uhm… I mean, did you make the chariot all alone?"

Ember nodded.

"What a talent." He fidgeted. Then he held out his free hand. "By the way, I'm Richard."

"Pleased to meet you." Ember took the hand, and an electrical burst zinged up her arms. "Ouch."

"Sorry." Richard blushed again. "I didn't mean to zap you. It's these daft shoes."

"No problem." Ember rubbed her arm to make the buzzing go away.

"Hey, would you like to come to the royal ball tomorrow night?" Richard looked right into her eyes, wearing his heart on his gaze. Ember could see how much he wanted her to say yes. Would her stepfather let her? Well, she could pretend she'd still have work to do. He'd readily believe her, especially since he wasn't really fond of making toys and would be glad to leave work to her. But what would she wear? "I can't. The only dress aside from my work clothes is my mother's wedding dress. And that one's way too old-fashioned to be acceptable as a ball gown."

"That's no problem at all." He pulled out a purse and handed her two gold coins and a silver one. "That should be enough to buy you a nice gown even on such short notice." He took her hand, bent forward and kissed it. Another zing ran up her arm, this time not from an electrical current. "I'm really looking forward to dancing with you. You're the first person I met who's also interested in magic." In an instant, he was gone, taking the packed carriage along and leaving a bag with the payment for the toy behind.

And I didn't even get to tell him my name, Ember thought. She heard the workroom door bang. Obviously Rose was back. Hurriedly she pocketed the coins Richard had given her and began to count the money in the bag he left as payment for the carriage.

"Did you see him?" Rose barged into the shop. "Did you?"

"Who?" Ember threw the last coin back into the bag. The pay was a little more than what her stepfather had asked.

"The crown prince's brother just left one of the shops next to ours. He passed our shop. You must have seen him!" Rose stared into the air with a look of bliss on her face that made her look stupid. "He'd be the right kind of husband for me… enough of everything to last me a lifetime. I'd be a princess!" She knuckled Ember's upper arm. "Why are you still here? Get out."

From long experience, Ember knew that Rose would take half of Richard's payment and claim Ember had taken it if she didn't rescue it, so she bit her lip and endured the slaps and pinches, grabbed the money bag and took it through to her stepfather.

For the rest of the day, Ember argued with herself. Should she buy a dress and go to the ball? She wasn't really the ball-going kind of girl.

At dusk, she was the last one left in the shop. As every evening, she was enjoying the peace and quiet as she closed the shutters and locked the doors, when a boy came running.

"Ma'am, wait a moment." He waved a piece of paper. Ember's heart skipped a beat. Had Richard sent a note? She took the note, handed the boy a copper as a reward, and locked the door behind him before she read the notice. It said:

I'll be with you for dinner,
Aunt Elizabeth

Ember groaned. Her stepfather's sister was even harder to bear than Rose. She'd have to hurry to get the evening meal done in time or Aunt Elizabeth would cuff her around the ears. Most likely she'd do that anyway.

Ember nearly ran home. In the market square, she wove her way through the crowd still buying from the stalls. Why were there still so many shoppers? It was close to dinner time. Usually the streets were nearly empty at this time of day. She stumbled over a dog on a leash, tried to regain her footing, and failed. With flailing arms, she fell head first onto the table of a curiosity stall. Luckily the table was a lot sturdier than most. A few smallish items and an empty birdcage fell to the ground.

"Oi! You're ruining my wares. You've got to pay for the damage." The stall owner did what every good merchant did under these circumstances – he tried to make money out of her. Ember growled as she righted herself. However, her threat of fetching the market guards if he tried to cheat her died on her lips when her gaze fell on the bird cage. A tiny woman in a frilly dress hugged the small branch someone had stuck between two bars with arms and legs. She was clearly trying not to fall off.

"What's that?" She pointed to the cage.

"It's a magical cage that will fulfill for you any wish if only you believe." The stall owner picked it up. "Some say a fairy was once trapped inside."

"She still is, as far as I can tell."

"Nonsense." The shop owner glared at her. "If there were someone inside, she'd be deprivation of personal freedom, and I'd never do that. The cage is empty."

Ember closed her mouth on her protest. If he didn't believe, all the better. "I want to buy it."

"What for?" All of a sudden, the merchant seemed suspicious.

"I'm invited to the royal ball." Ember batted her eyelashes like she'd seen Lilly do at her admirers. "And any luck concerning the perfect husband is well appreciated."

The merchant seemed to be satisfied by her answer. "Five gold coins."

"Five? For an empty cage? I'll give you one." Ember knew she was expected to barter, and she did her best considering time was running out. In the end, she got the cage for two gold pieces. That left her with the silver coin.

As Ember hurried on with the cage in her hands, she thought, *I need to show the fairy to Richard. He'll be so delighted.* A sudden dread made her stop. *If I want to meet him, I'll have to go to the ball, and I've got nothing to wear and not enough money left to buy a decent dress!* Her gaze fell on a stall a little ahead that sold ribbons and fabric. She was quite decent with a needle, so maybe she could alter her mother's wedding dress after all. She spent her remaining money on lace, ribbons and frills.

Back home, she set her shopping and the cage on the table in her room.

"I'll get back to you right after dinner," she said to the fairy. "But if I don't hurry now, I'll get into big trouble."

The tiny fairy didn't react. She clung to her seat as if her life depended on it. With a shrug, Ember hurried off toward the kitchen.

"I tell you, that girl will be the death of you one day," Aunt Elizabeth announced as Ember walked in with the soup. She was sure that if she hadn't been carrying the tureen, the old lady would have slapped her, so she stayed out of her way as best she could while she served dinner.

"Shut up, Liz." Her stepfather's scowl deepened. "You don't understand what she means to us."

"Oh, I understand that very well." The woman's perfume wafted into Ember's nose, and she struggled not to sneeze.

"I beg your pardon?" As she turned to her father, Rose's voice sounded like raised eyebrows although she'd never mar her features that way. "In what regard do we care for ... her?" She shot Ember a glance filled with disgust.

"Go and fetch the next course," the stepfather said to Ember. He waited deliberately until she had left the room, so Ember hurried into the adjoining room where the ventilation shafts connected both rooms.

"...in front of her." Her stepfather's voice sounded angry. "You can hate her all you want, but you will be as friendly as you can manage."

19

"That's unbelievable!" Rose's repugnance was palatable. "You should dump her at the next orphanage or work house as soon as possible."

Ember shivered. Why did Rose hate her so much? After all, she was the general dogsbody around here while Rose more or less did what she wanted all day long. Holding her breath, Ember waited for her stepfather's answer. For a while, it seemed as if he wouldn't speak, but then she heard the floorboards creak and realized that he must have made sure she wasn't listening at the door. What luck that he didn't remember the ventilation system. Well, she was the one who had to clean it. He never bothered with household chores.

"You will be friendly to her whether you like it or not. Do you think I'm happy to be burdened with her?" Her stepfather's voice was dangerously low, but she could still understand him for the silence in the other room. "Her mother left the shop, all her money, and the house to her. I am nothing but her guardian and have to prove in court once a year that I'm not spending her money uselessly. If we get rid of her, we'll be beggars in the street in less than a day. If she dies unexpectedly, the house will be turned into an orphanage in her memory with us as the servants of I-don't-know-how-many brats. Don't you think I've considered my options ever since her mother died? But the bitch knew me too well. My wife has closed every darn loophole I could think of."

Ember was dumbstruck. She owned everything? She? Not her stepfather? She was so shocked that she nearly missed Aunt Elizabeth talking, but the loudness of her voice pierced Ember's stupor.

"Well, that will not be a concern for you for much longer." Aunt Elizabeth sounded stern and secretly pleased. Ember could easily imagine the superior smile with the arched eyebrows on her face. "Because I have some good news... No, I won't tell you yet. Let's talk about that over dessert."

"What is it?" Rose asked. Ember left her to cajole her aunt and hurried to the kitchen to fetch the main course before someone wondered what was taking her so long.

After serving dessert, she hurried back into the adjoining room. She was as curious as Rose about her aunt's announcement. Maybe her "good news" meant something good for Ember too, for once. Holding her breath, she listened.

"Well, Liz, what did you mean to tell us?"

"You're just as impatient as your daughter, Ambrose. Why isn't Lilly at home today? This concerns her too."

"She's visiting a friend. I can fetch her if I know what to tell her." The eagerness in Rose's voice was unmistakable.

"Alright. I'll tell you." The aunt made a pause that stretched into a seemingly endless silence. Ember could practically see Rose shifting on her seat impatiently. Finally, the aunt spoke again. "By the end of this year, both you and Lilly will be married to rich nobles, or even to one of the princes, because I managed to secure two invitations to the royal ball tonight."

Rose's squeal nearly burst Ember's eardrums and swallowed the rest of what her aunt said.

"Oh, there's so much to do... I need a new dress... and pearls! And better shoes... and..." Rose's voice faded away as she hurried toward her room. Ember peeked through the door to make sure no one followed her and then hurried downstairs to the kitchen. The moment she arrived, the bell rang, calling her back to the dining room. With a sigh, she followed the call.

"We're invited to the royal ball, my dear. Fetch Lilly. Now. Hurry!" Aunt Elizabeth shooed her away. "We've only got three hours left."

Ember did as she was told. She didn't begrudge Lilly the pleasure of going to the ball, and with the family busy, she might get a chance to make changes to her mother's wedding dress.

Half an hour later, she carried Lilly's overnight bag into her sister's room.

"I still think it's unfair that you can't come," Lilly said. "I could give you one of my dresses. You're so much smaller than I am, it should fit you perfectly. And you so deserve a nice husband. Someone who can take you away from Rose."

Ember appreciated Lilly's concern, but she only shrugged. "It's not that bad."

"I know it is." Lilly smiled at her. "I'll put in a good word with Aunty."

"She won't allow it, and I'm not really interested in going to a ball anyway." Ember didn't want Lilly to draw attention to her. She needed to get her dress done, and time was ticking. "You'd better get dressed. Your aunt bought new dressed for both you and Rose."

But her stepsister remained stubborn. "I'll make sure you're coming along. Even if it's only for watching from the sidelines." She hurried to Rose's room, where her aunt and her sister were busy selecting the right accessories to go with the new dress, while Ember's stepfather stood around, a little forlorn. Lilly didn't bother greeting anyone. "Aunty dearest. I want Ember to come along."

"What for? To embarrass you in that..." – she waved at Ember's work clothes – "... dress?"

"She can have one of my older ones. But she's our sister and has the right to go too." Lilly cocked her head and smiled, a gesture that always made everyone do her bidding. But her aunt seemed immune.

"I don't see how we can smuggle her in. I've only got two invitations."

"Daddy... please?" Lilly grabbed her father's arm.

He sighed. "Very well, my dear." He grabbed a bowl with pearls from Rose's nightstand, maybe a broken necklace, marched out of the room and into his late wife's bedroom – untouched since her death – and emptied the pearls into the cold fireplace. Ashes billowed up, covering the wooden floorboards in a wide circle. He turned to Ember. "If you manage to clean the room and collect all the pearls back into the bowl, I'll find a way for you to come along."

"Thank you, sir." Ember bowed, secretly relieved for this easy way out. She'd clean the room as soon as she got her dress done. The pearls could wait for tomorrow.

"But Dad!" Lilly's protest remained unheard. Her father had already walked away.

"Get dressed, Lilly," he called back over his shoulder. "You've only got two hours left."

"That's so unfair!" Lilly sobbed.

"Don't worry about me. I can find the pearls easily." Ember patted her hand and pulled her back toward her room. "I'll be done in no time. You'll see."

"The ball won't be much fun if only half the family will be there." Lilly sniffed but her tears had stopped.

"You know I hate balls. Give me a good smithy or an hour at the toy shop. That makes me happy." Ember pushed her through the door. "Please, Lilly, believe me. I'm much happier if I don't have to go."

"Promise you'll try to get the pearls collected." Lilly obviously still wasn't listening.

Ember sighed. "Yes, Lilly. I will. Now, you hurry to get dressed or Rose will leave without you."

"Fine." Lilly shuffled into her room, looking around as if in a daze. But Ember couldn't stay. Time was running short already.

She hurried to the kitchen to fetch her mechanical broom, an invention her real father had made before he died. A tiny, steam-drive turbine created enough suction to draw light muck like ashes, small stones, or dust into a collecting box below the handle. As fast as she could, she returned to her mother's room to suck up the ashes on the ground and from the fireplace. The pearls clattered into the box. She'd sieve them out tomorrow. She had more important things to do right now.

Taking the mechanical broom along, she hurried to her room, where her gaze fell on the fairy in the cage.

"Oh dear, I nearly forgot about you. Are you hungry?" Ember opened a small wooden box on her wobbly table and pulled out a slightly crumpled apple. The fairy nodded eagerly, so she cut the apple into slices and put them into the cage through the bars. Then she opened her wardrobe to take out her mother's wedding dress, and jolted back in surprise.

A dark blue dress with a low neckline, puffy arms, and a wide crinoline hung beside the wedding dress and a fitting pair of shoes below. Trust Lilly to pick the perfect dress for her. Ember felt a surge of gratefulness sweep through her. The color would go very well with her auburn hair. Only, Lilly's shoes were several sizes too small.

Someone knocked at the door. Since only Lilly respected her privacy, Ember called and her sister came in. "I found a string of pearls in my jewel box that'd go nicely with the dress. Come on, I'll help you to get dressed."

Ember had an idea. After all, Lilly would recognize the dress if she showed up in it anyway. She took her sister's hands. "Listen, Lilly. I'm not going to come with you. I was invited by the second son of a lesser noble this morning myself, but I don't want Rose to know."

"Oooooh!" Lilly squealed, but slapped a hand over her mouth immediately. She continued in a whisper. "Is he your beau?"

"Not at all, but we share some interests, and he wanted to dance with me." Ember hoped she wasn't blushing. The idea of Richard as a beau seemed absurd, although she had to admit that his soft brown eyes were still vivid in her memory.

"If he asked you to come to the royal ball, he fancies you. Trust me." Lilly smiled. "I'm not a very bright girl, I know, but I do know men."

"You're perfect the way you are. At least your heart is in the right place." Ember hugged her. "I sometimes think Rose has lost hers."

Lilly giggled. "Come on, let me help you with your dress. Dad will be calling me any minute."

With stifled laughs, Ember allowed Lilly to help her into the dress. Her sister even came up with the idea of using a tiara and tying a midnight blue see-through scarf to it, so she could hide her face in case she got too close to Rose.

"Rose never remembers my dresses," Lilly said when Ember mentioned the possibility. "By the way, why do you have an empty cage on your table?"

"Oh that..." Ember thought frantically for a good excuse, only wondering for a very short moment why she could see the fairy and nobody else could. "I bought a nightbird from my savings, but it wouldn't sing and looked so sad that I let it go."

"Oh yes, nightbirds are delicate creatures." And off Lilly went on a tangent of thought about birds in general and singing birds in captivity. Ember only half listened.

"Lilly! Where are you? We're leaving in five minutes!" The voice of Ember's stepfather boomed through the house as if magnified. Hurriedly Lilly hugged Ember and ran out of her room. Five minutes later, several doors banged and then the house fell silent. Ember sighed with relief. Now all she needed to do was find a pair of shoes that would go with the dress and somehow smuggle the cage into the palace. She hesitated. Maybe it was better to slip in without the cage and get Richard to come out to look at it.

"Hey, will you let me out sometime soon?" The fairy sat on an apple slice, dangling her feet. "I'll grant you a wish if you do."

The voice sounded just as loud as a human's, which caught Ember by surprise. When she regained her composure, she said, "I'm not interested in getting wishes granted. Thank you."

"Why else did you buy me then? I know you can see me, so don't deny that."

"Of course I can see you. Why shouldn't I?"

"You believe in magic and in fairies. Your sister doesn't, so she can't see me. It's as easy as that. Now let me out." The fairy fluttered her wings.

"I can't. I need to take you to the royal ball tonight."

"I knew it." The fairy sighed. "But let me tell you that I cannot make someone fall in love with you. That's outside my competence. All I can do is make sure that the circumstances are right."

"I told you I don't need that." Ember felt more tempted than she liked to admit. Deep down in her heart, she would have given a lot if the fairy had made Richard fall for her... at least a little. But that wasn't what she was planning to do. "I want to show you to someone who is interested in magic. He will know what we need to do with you."

"It's easy. Just set me free, and I'll find my way home."

Ember shook her head. "Everyone knows how dangerous mechanics are for magical creatures. I remember Mother telling me tales of house-friends and spider-kings, of trolls in the North and windbrides in the South. Most of them are gone now. I can't risk you like that."

"So what are you planning to do?" The fairy stood up and balanced on the apple, trying not to touch the cage's foundation.

"I'd like to send you to a place where magic still exists. But I've never even been outside of this town, so I wouldn't know where to send you to. But Richard will. I'm sure of that."

"Fine." The fairy hovered over the apple slices now. "Let me out, and I promise I'll stay with you until you've spoken to that Richard of yours."

Ember considered the proposition. It'd be a lot easier to get to the palace if she didn't have to lug around a cage that looked empty to most people. But did she dare trust a fairy's promise?

"What if I accept its promise and it still flies away?" she thought out loud without noticing.

"I wouldn't do that." The fairy shook her wings, which made her flight a little more wobbly. "Most magical creatures are bound by their word. So if I make a promise, it's as good as an oath from a human."

"In that case…" Hesitantly, Ember opened the cage, and the fairy shot out like oiled lightning.

She stretched, and stretched, and stretched, growing bigger all the time. When she was about the same size as Ember, she sighed. "It's such a relief to not be tiny anymore."

"If you can grow this big, why didn't you break out of the cage before?" Ember stared at her, wide-eyed.

"I made a stupid promise a long time ago." The fairy looked around. "Well, how do we get to the palace? In a pumpkin?"

Ember thought of the carriage Richard had fetched that morning and giggled.

"We'll need some decent transportation." The fairy took her hand and pulled her downstairs. On the stairs, she glanced at Ember's bare feet. "And shoes. Decent-sized shoes. My, your feet are on the big side, aren't they?"

"It comes in handy when I have to run," Ember said, still giggling.

They hurried through the kitchen into the yard, which was dominated by a pile of broken toys.

"What? No vegetables?" The fairy looked around in confusion. "But every damsel in distress has a vegetable garden."

"For one, I'm not a damsel in distress. And second, no one in town has a vegetable garden anymore. That's what farmers are for. They sell you the goods you need."

"All good and fine, but now where will I get a pumpkin I can turn into a carriage?"

Ember picked up a black toy coach. It was still functional, if missing its horse. "If you can make this a little bigger, I'll ask the neighbor for his pony."

"Ah yes, that'll do nicely." The fairy waved a wand she'd pulled from her voluminous skirt. "And don't you worry about a horse, my dear." She whistled, and three pigeons came and landed at her feet. She touched them with the wand, and they changed into a horse and two men in livery – well, they were *more or less* human and horse. Big, white wings adorned their shoulder blades, and they looked big enough to carry them skywards.

As much as Ember liked the look of the winged horse and men, she knew they'd draw too much attention. "Can't you take off the wings?"

"Nope. That'd take away their chance to become pigeons again. But I can make them invisible." The fairy waved her wand again, and the wings vanished. Only now and again, something white fluttered in her peripheral vision, and the occasional feather drifted to the ground.

Next, the fairy touched the toy coach, and it grew to a decent-sized landau. It's cape hood was folded back. With a flurry of wings and a hop, the fairy took a seat. Ember climbed in the traditional way, aided by one of the men in livery.

"Oh, I forgot your shoes." The fairy pointed at Ember's feet, and her sturdy workman's boots transformed into bluish, sparkling glass slippers.

"Won't they break when I walk on them?" Ember asked.

"Not one bit. Deep inside they still know that they're boots."

"So it's more an illusion than a real transformation?"

"Real transformations take a lot more magical energy, and in this town there isn't much to have. I spent most on the birds." The fairy waved her wand a last time. "Now, let's get to that palace of yours."

The tiny door in the garden stretched like a person waking up. It stretched until it was big enough for the landau to pass through. The horse began to trot.

Ten minutes later, they reached the palace's courtyard. A twang of sadness shot through Ember at the knowledge that the ride was over for now. One pigeon-man helped her out of the coach, while the fairy flew again. Ember watched the landau roll to the assigned parking lot. Most other places were filled with steam-cars.

"What are you waiting for?" asked the fairy. "We haven't got all night."

Ember lifted her skirts a little and hurried up the stairs. At the top, a line of guests still waited to be admitted. The girls at the front showed their invitation to the guards, who examined them for weapons and let them in. Before Ember could worry about her oral invitation, a young man hurried toward her.

"What a magnificent dress, milady," He took her hand and led her past the guards, who acknowledged him with a curt nod. At a lower voice he said, "Richard told me to fetch you. I'm his valet and his best friend. Who's that winged lady following us?"

"You can see her too?" Ember's eyes grew wide. She hadn't expected to meet another person aside from Richard who still believed in fairies. "I thought she'd be invisible to everyone except me."

"I'm only invisible to those who do not believe in magic," the fairy said without lowering her voice.

"And there aren't many believers in this town. That's one reason why it's so hard to do magic here." She sighed. "I wish we would be done with this so I can go home. There's so little magic around, I feel as if I'm shriveling."

Ember stared at her but couldn't find a trace of aging or shrinking. Maybe the fairy was overly dramatic. Still, there was a haunted look to her that hadn't been there when she had been in the birdcage.

"This way." The valet turned a corner to a corridor leading away from the sounds of the ballroom. Ember was secretly relieved. One less chance to bump into Rose, Aunt Elizabeth, or her step-father. They turned another corner, walked up and down several stairs and around more corners. Soon Ember could neither say from which direction they had come nor on which floor they were. Finally, a big, single door loomed ahead.

"Richard will be inside." The valet opened the door far enough to let her through. "I will take my leave now. Servants aren't welcome at the ball." Before Ember realized that she was entering the ballroom from a side door, he pushed her and the fairy through and closed the door behind her.

In front of her stood the pavilion for the royals, draped with red curtains which also shielded Ember from most of the ballroom. She looked around for Richard. Several courtiers scurried to and fro in the space between her and the curtains, and from the other side a loud voice announced the arriving visitors.

Gentle music played somewhere up above, but Ember couldn't see enough to pinpoint the exact location.

"A fair maiden like you shouldn't hide in the back like this." A man with a face like a speckled egg and hair like white feathers grabbed her hand and pulled her toward the ballroom. "Do me the honor of dancing with me."

Ember tried to free her hand, but the man held it in a grip of steel. Obviously the valet had made a mistake and Richard wasn't here after all.

"I'm sorry to disappoint you, cousin, but this is my dance partner." Richard's hand grabbed his cousin's wrist. "Let go or…"

"Or what, substitute prince?" The white-haired youth sneered at Richard.

"As long as I'm my father's son, you'd better obey."

Although the fact that Richard had to be the king's second son shocked her, Ember marveled at his calm demeanor. She felt like screaming. Richard took a step forward. With a snort, the man let go of Ember's hand, and she relaxed with a sigh of relief. Richard took her hand and kissed it like only a prince could.

"I am delighted that you managed to accept my invitation." His eyes shone as he looked at her, and Ember's heart sped up. He stepped closer and said, "You look marvelous. Nearly as beautiful as this morning."

"You…" Ember swallowed as if she had to stop her racing heart from escaping though her throat. "You thought me beautiful in my workdress?"

"It suits you even better than this evening dress."

He stood close enough to Ember that she breathed his smell of cinnamon and oranges. For a moment, Ember wished she had agreed to the fairy's wish-granting idea. But then she remembered that love couldn't be achieved by magic. She sighed and took a step back. Richard looked up in surprise and noticed the fairy, who still stood at the door, tapping her foot.

"Who is the lovely lady in the pink gown you brought along?" Richard looked straight at the fairy. "It's surprising that my cousin didn't try to snatch her instead of you. He's usually much more interested in ethereal-looking women."

"Thank you for the compliment, young man." The fairy stepped closer and allowed Richard to kiss her hand too. "I'm Fayrula, and your cousin couldn't see me." Again she explained about her invisibility to unbelievers. "And this little girl here said you could get me home in a way that will stop me from getting harmed by all the gadgets this country is using everywhere."

"You've found proof for magic! Thank you so much." Richard grabbed Ember's waist and swung her around. "Now Father *must* believe me."

"You forget that he can't see her," Ember said, feeling strange for talking to the prince like they were pals.

"He has to. I need his permission to start my expedition."

"Your expedition?" Fayrula's and Ember's voices overlapped, creating a beautiful harmony.

"I've been planning an expedition to study magic for quite a while," Richard said. "However, my father is worried that I'll run into trouble and won't let me go. After all, my elder brother is so ill, it's unlikely he'll ever recover." A shadow crossed his brow, which he dismissed with a shrug, but Ember had noticed it even though he continued to speak in a seemingly happy voice. "Father needs me as the new heir."

"Heir?" Panic wafted through Ember's brain, draining her of her strength. Her fingers grew cold and her stomach knotted. "*You* are the crown prince?" She couldn't fall for the crown prince! A second son of a king would have been close to impossible, but no way a crown prince would ever marry a common toy maker, not even if he wanted to which was still unclear.

"Replacement crown prince," Richard said and shrugged. "But I'm not interested. My studies are far more important, don't you think? Imagine all the things we can discover if only we set out! Unicorns, dragons, windbrides, trolls, maybe even some unknown creatures."

"There are plenty of dangerous ones around," Fayrula interjected.

"Oh, I'll take my valet along. He's as good as I am with his sword. Between the two of us, we'll cope."

"If you take me home, I'll grant you a wish," the fairy said, louder than before. "A single one, mind." She held out a hand, and Ember could see the eagerness on her face. Before Richard could take her outstretched hand, Ember pulled him aside.

"Think about it before you agree."

"Here you are, my prince." An elderly man in a black robe grabbed the prince's arm. "Introductions are over; you must open the ball now. Ah, I see you've already got a beautiful dance partner. Hurry now." He pushed Ember and the prince along in front of him with surprising strength.

Everything inside of Ember screamed, but with Richard holding her hand and the stranger pushing her, there wasn't much she could do. Hurriedly she let down her veil.

"Why a veil?" Richard whispered. They were just pushed past the curtained area, and he nodded to his parents in passing. Ember felt as if she was using two left legs as she attempted a curtsy. When the black-clad man let go, Richard pulled her along, still insisting on an answer. "The veil?"

"My stepfamily is somewhere in the room, and I'd prefer not to be recognized."

"I understand." Richard stopped in the middle of the open space in the ballroom's center. The music started and they took their first steps. To her great surprise, Ember fell in as if dancing was second nature to her. Not once did she step on Richard's toes.

He smiled down at her. "Now, why didn't you want me to accept Fayrula's offer?"

"By all I know, which is fairly little, fairies stick very closely to the terms they agree on. So if you accept her current offer, you'd have to take her with you, and then she'll grant you a wish."

"So?" Richard swung her around the room in rhythm to the music, and Ember felt like she was flying. More couples joined the dance.

"You should try to get her to agree on the other way round. The wish first, and then the expedition." Ember was very aware of his hand on her bare back. Maybe the deep neckline hadn't been such a great idea after all. Heat spread from his hand through her body, and she began to sweat. The more couples danced with them, the smaller the world seemed to grow. Still, she managed to keep focused on the idea she had before they were forced to dance. "If she agrees to the reverse order, you can ask her to heal your brother. If his heir is restored, your father will probably be more lenient when you ask him for permission to go on an expedition."

Richard's face lit up like a whole chandelier. His mouth opened and closed as if he didn't know what to say. When the music ended, he pulled her through the throng to one of the double doors leading outside. Hands reached for them and people called out for his attention, but he brushed them all aside in an extremely polite manner. A woman pushed herself right in front of the prince and batted her eyelashes at him.

It was Rose.

Ember froze.

"Would you do me the honor of dancing with me, Your Majesty?" Rose pressed closer to Richard, as if pushed by the people around her. Her ample bosom dug into the prince's chest, giving in just the right places.

Standing a little to the side of Richard, Ember could see the telltale blush on his face. Her heart plummeted. No man was able to withstand a bosom like that. From the corner of her eye, she recognized Aunt Elizabeth's confident grin and her stepfather's prideful posture. Her shoulders slumped, and she missed the prince's answer, but she followed when he pulled her forward. As soon as he dumped her politely somewhere at the fringe of the crowd, she'd return home. What had she been thinking in coming in the first place? She should have made the connection between the visit to her shop and Rose's remark about the prince earlier. It would have saved her a lot of heartache.

"You shouldn't hide your beauty like that, milady." Her veil ripped and hung limply from Richard's cousin's hand. Instinctively, Ember freed her hand from Richard's grip and put them over her face. She turned away from where she remembered her family standing and hurried onward. The doors to the outside were only a few more steps away.

Cold air streamed into her lungs as she left the ballroom. She stood on a balcony spanning half of the palace's front. The city spread out into the night and its streetlights made it look as if it was studded with diamonds. A hand grabbed her shoulder and turned her around. Richard? Ember's heart thumped so hard, he had to repeat his question.

"Are you alright?"

She nodded. She was, now. How could he not be dancing with Rose though? "What about my stepsister?" It occurred to her that he wouldn't know who she was talking about, so she added, "The girl who asked you to dance."

Richard's face contorted. "What a pompous, self-centered dullard. As if I'd dance with the likes of her. Anyone could see at first glance that she was already deeply in love… with herself. I've met her like once too often." When he looked down at Ember again, his features softened. "I much prefer someone intelligent enough to save me from a stupid mistake while simultaneously thinking of a way to save my brother."

Ember's knees wobbled. She didn't have the strength to evade him as he slowly lowered his face. When their lips met, elation shot through her like lightning, or like those colored explosives people loved to burn on birthdays. He liked her, maybe even loved her… Her blood sang, and she lifted her arms to wrap them around his neck, but before she could complete her move, a human steam engine slammed into her side, screaming like a boiling kettle.

"That's my prince, you imbecile!"

Rose's fingernails left long gashes on Ember's chest, but worst of all, she felt herself slipping over the balcony's railing. Frantically she grabbed for something, anything she could hold on to, but there was nothing. She saw Richard's outstretched hands above her, heard guards' heavy steps running toward the balcony, and saw Rose stare after her with a smug grin on her face. Fear lanced through Ember, pushing aside the slight pain from the gashes on her chest. Everything inside of her screamed for help.

Something pink appeared beside her and time stopped. She was no longer hurtling toward the ground. Relief flooded through her like a wave, washing away all other emotions.

"Since you seem to be the only sensible person around here, I'll take my chances with you. Make the prince accept my bargain and you'll live." All of a sudden, Fayrula seemed much older than before. Her skin had a gray sheen and her pink dress looked limp. Whatever she was doing obviously strained her a lot.

Accepting her help was the sensible thing to do but Ember couldn't help but try. "I'll get him to agree if you're a little flexible on the conditions."

"I won't grant him more than one wish. It's hard enough already." Fayrula was clearly sweating.

"Change the order. First the wish, then the expedition, and you've got a deal." For a moment, Ember feared the fairy would not agree and let her continue her fall, but then she nodded and whistled. Once.

White wings opened and two men shot toward them. Time resumed its normal pace. Before Ember could do so much as open her mouth to scream, the men caught her and flew with her over the roofs of the town. Ember closed her mouth and looked back. She noticed that Fayrula flipped the prince one of her glass slippers before she followed.

They landed in the yard of her house. Ember's knees shook so much she had to sit down. She didn't care one bit that the beautiful dress got dusty. "Thank you."

"Gurrr," said one of the pigeon angels. He and his friend dissolved and became pigeons again just as the town hall bell started ringing midnight.

Ember laughed until she cried. When she didn't stop, Fayrula slapped her.

"What's wrong with you?" she asked. "Don't you know you've got a job to do?"

"I know." Ember tried to calm down, with only little success. "But this is... you know, it is like a silly fairy tale. The unwanted stepdaughter attends the prince's ball, draws his attention, and leaves at the stroke of midnight. Are you sure you didn't meddle?"

Fayrula smiled and settled beside Ember. "I wish I had, but there's so little magic in the air here that I couldn't have, even if I had wanted. But sometimes, magic creates itself from nothing. That's what distinguishes it from your technical energies."

"So you're saying that this evening created magic?"

"Without it I wouldn't have had the strength to save you."

Ember was dumbstruck.

"Can we go back to your room now?" Fayrula looked so tired that Ember wondered if she'd make it up all those stairs. The fairy stood up and held out her hand. "I need to get back into the cage."

"Why is that?" Ember got up without Fayrula's help.

"I don't know how it works, but as long as I don't touch the bars, the cage seems to have kept me from being influenced by technology too much." Fayrula walked toward the house, growing smaller with every step.

"You mean like a lightning cage?" Ember picked her up and hurried inside and up the stairs.

"Whatever that is." Fayrula curled up in her hand and fell asleep. In passing, Ember snatched a feather cushion from the sofa in the top floor hall, hurried to her room, stuffed it into the cage and placed the fairy very gently on it. Hopefully that'd be enough to save her magical friend. Since she didn't want Fayrula to feel imprisoned again when she woke, she left the door of the cage open.

Then she undressed and climbed into her own bed. With all her might, Ember wished for a magical healing of the fairy. She did her best to believe in it, but the day had been exhausting, and she fell asleep soon.

She woke from slamming doors and loud screaming.

"You were darn lucky, Rose." That was her stepfather.

"I didn't do anything. That prince imagined things. He's insane. You've got to sue the king."

"If you don't shut your gap this minute, I'll personally apply a verdict to your rear!"

And so it went. A timid knock at the door forced Ember to sit up. She knew who it was. "Come in, Lilly."

"Oh God, I'm so glad you're still alive." Her sister rushed in and hugged her. Tears ran over her face, and she hiccuped. "I don't know how you did it, but... oh dear... I was so worried when I saw you topple over the balustrade..."

"Why didn't they lock Rose away?" Ember didn't really want to see her stepsister in jail, but she wondered.

"When they couldn't find your body, everyone assumed that I had misinterpreted something." Lilly sat up straight and wiped her face.

"What about Rich... the prince? He witnessed everything."

"He seemed pretty preoccupied with some sort of shoe." Lilly shook her head. "He held it in his hands and looked over the town's roofs as if bespelled."

Smiling, Ember sank back into her cushion. "Thanks for forcing me to go. I had a great time until Rose pushed me."

Lilly cocked her head. "Did you get hurt when you hit the ground?"

"Not much, I was lucky." Ember didn't like lying to her but she was sure Lilly would never believe the truth.

"I'm so glad. What would I have done without you...?" Already Lilly's thoughts wandered to a new subject. "You know what? I met a young noble at the ball, and he's oh so cute. What's even better, he fancies me and asked me out to dine with him tomorrow."

"That's great news." Ember sat up again. She'd noticed that the fairy was waking and was wondering how she could get Lilly to leave when her stepfather's voice boomed from downstairs.

"Lilly, come here right now! Hurry. This might be our last chance." He seemed extremely excited. "Rose, to your room."

"But he's *my* prince, and I've got the most dainty feet."

Ember swung her feet out of the bed and walked with Lilly to the balustrade that separated the top floor from the entrance hall. She looked down as far as she could but there wasn't enough light to see all of the big hall. "What's all this about?"

"I told you the prince was preoccupied with a shoe. A glass slipper." Lilly walked downstairs, deliberately slow. "He swore he'd marry the girl whose foot fitted into that shoe."

"So?"

"The minute he did that, the shoe began to walk toward the city... well, hop would be more correct. It must be quite an advanced bit of technology." Lilly waved at her with a sad smile. "Now Rose has put all her hope on it stopping here, and Aunty Liz promised to send word as soon as it neared our street. And you know how Dad always does what Rose asks him to do."

When Lilly was halfway down the stairs, Ember returned to her room and began to dress in her usual work clothes, musing. She looked at the fairy, who was just now rubbing her tiny eyes. "That was your doing, wasn't it?"

"Well, I had to ensure your prince would find you so you can agree on the details." Fayrula yawned. "I need to go home. I've been away for far too long."

Strong fists banged against the front door in the downstairs hall. They reverberated up to Ember's room. The voice of Ember's stepfather drifted up to her as he opened personally. She wondered why there was no sound from Rose. Maybe she was still dressing up for the occasion.

Ember tied the laces of her remaining boot and hurried downstairs with Fayrula on her shoulder. *Richard has come.* She marveled at how happy this thought made her she hurried down the steps of the staircase.

She stopped when she could see the scene below. Several guards and servants in livery blocked the wide open door. Richard stood beside his valet, who carried a velvet cushion. He just went down on his knee to offer the glass slipper.

"Here's one of my daughters." Ember's stepfather pushed Lilly forward, who looked as if she'd swallowed a newt. "The other will be with us any minute. The shoe is hers. Unfortunately, the second one broke on the way home. We had to ditch the shards."

A figure swept past Ember, and Rose's elbow dug into her side. She gasped.

"Stay out of my way," Rose hissed as she sailed down the last flight of stairs. Close to the hall, she spoke louder. "How nice of you to bring me my shoe." She lifted her skirt, exposing a dainty foot in a white stocking.

"You don't look one bit like the girl I'm looking for." Richard's voice was low and strained. "In fact, you remind me of the harpy who attacked the woman I love. I'd rather let your sister here try the shoe than believe it's yours."

Richard's words fell like stones and were followed by an uncomfortable silence. Ember felt her heart go out to him. And to Lilly. She knew that her sister would be deeply unhappy if the shoe fit her. But the shoe had a mind of its own. It broke free from the valet's grasp and began hopping up the stairs, transforming as it went. With every step, it looked less like a glass slipper and more like her second boot. Ember smiled. She couldn't help it.

Rose tried to grab the shoe but with her tied waist and the wide skirt, she didn't have a chance. The shoe evaded her easily. Gingerly Ember walked downstairs until she reached her shoe. Then she lifted the rim of her work dress and showed the matching one. The enchanted shoe toppled and lay still.

"I've still got the second one, Richard."

"Dearest!" The relief in Richard's voice was very evident.

Rose screamed with rage and turned to attack Ember again, but this time she was prepared. She dove under her sister's arm and hurried down the last few steps.

Without concern for decency, the prince ran forward to meet her. He wrapped his arms around her and hugged her so hard she could barely breathe. From the corner of her eye, she saw Rose launch another attack, but before she could reach the couple, two guards caught her and held her struggling, screaming form.

"Take her outside." Richard's gaze stayed on Ember. "Maybe she'll cool down then."

He kissed Ember's hair and whispered, "When I saw the angels I was absolutely sure you were dead, but then the shoe insisted on walking. I… I hovered between despair and hope. Never, *ever* do that to me again. Promise?"

His arms hugged her even stronger, and Ember gasped for air.

"Can't breathe." When he let her go, she laughed. "I'm so happy to see you too." She pointed to the fairy. "I think it's time to take her home, don't you?"

"Since my brother is going to die in a few months, my problem is still the same."

"Your father didn't start to believe in magic when he saw a shoe walk on its own?" Ember's smile grew even wider. "What a stubborn fool. So it's all the better that you've got me."

His eyebrows rose questioningly.

"I convinced the fairy that she needs to grant you a wish before you can travel. If her magic suffices, she'll heal your brother. Then you will be allowed to travel. After all, your father promised, right?"

For a second, Richard stood paralyzed. Then he grabbed Ember's face with both hands and kissed her. Instantly, Ember felt as if she were on fire. She wrapped her arms around him and returned the kiss with fervor. When they finally came up for air, Richard took her hands and asked, "Will you marry me?"

Something burst inside of Ember's chest and radiated through her body as if the world could never be wrong again. Despite the biggest smile she'd ever worn on her face, she shook her head. "Are you crazy? We only met a day ago, and you don't even know my name yet. Don't you think we should get to know each other a little bit before we get married?"

Reluctantly, he nodded. "What do you suggest?"

"For one, my name is Emberlin but everyone calls me Ember. You may too. And secondly, I'd love to come along on your expedition." Holding her breath, Ember waited for an answer. She found it in his eyes that shone with happiness.

After a long silence, they walked down the rest of the stairs hand in hand.

"We'll need the cage from my room. It seems to protect the fairy somewhat," Ember said, and Richard told his valet to fetch it. Amber asked, "Are we going to travel by horse or by coach?"

"If you don't mind, I'd prefer horses," Richard said. "Will you be able to keep up with us?"

"Congratulations, Ember." Lilly was the first to speak. "I know how much an expedition like this means to you. You've always been the dreamer in our family."

Secretly amused by Lilly's awed expression, Ember hugged her. Then she turned to her stepfather. "By the way, as I found out just recently, this is my house, not yours. I want Rose out of it by noon. Lilly and you can stay, but Rose will never set a foot into my house or into my shop again. Do we understand each other?"

Her stepfather's jaw opened and closed but no sound came out.

"You will work in the back of my shop and keep it stocked. I'll pay you an allowance that should cover your living costs, as long as my trustee reports that you're working well." Ember turned to Lilly. "Would you be interested in taking care of the shop in my place until I return?"

"Can my beau help if he wants? When I told him yesterday that you own a toy shop, his eyes grew all dreamy."

Ember nodded and hugged her again.

"Where shall Rose go?" Suddenly, her stepfather sounded distraught. "She's my daughter too."

"Send her to Aunt Elizabeth. They deserve each other." Ember turned to her prince. "And now, let's go and save your brother. We've got an expedition to plan."

Bonus Story: The Goat's Curse
based loosely on "The Wishing-Table, The Gold-Ass, and The Cudgel in the Sack".

Frank put the finishing touches on the cake he'd made for his brother. Six slices of bread had gone into it, as well as raisins, a baked egg 'n milk pancake, a little bit of the jam they still had from last year, and a dollop of Father's self-made Schnapps. They couldn't afford a full manhood feast but today Gerd would turn sixteen, so they had to have at least something.

"What a pity that Otto isn't with us," his father said as he came in and dumped a pile of logs beside the open fireplace. Logs they'd sorely miss during the winter. "I miss him a lot."

Frank refrained from asking why he had sent his eldest brother away in the first place. As often as he'd put the question to his father, he'd never gotten a satisfactory answer. He set the small candle on top of the cake that he'd bought with one of their last coppers when the door opened with a crash.

"I'm back! And just before the rain set in." Gerd always talked as if they were living in a giant house, but this time the goat's bleating nearly drowned out his voice. After hanging up his felt hat, he turned to take the animal to its pen at the far side of the tiny living room, and Frank lit the candle.

"Wait." Father grabbed Gerd's arm and pulled him and the goat back to the fire. "Did you feed the goat well?"

Frank frowned. Father had never asked that before, and Gerd had herded the goat ever since Otto left.

"I need to know if you fed the goat well!" Father stared at Gerd as if his life depended on it. Frank noticed a red flicker in his eyes, probably the reflection of the fire in the hearth.

"Sure did." Gerd grinned. "I took her to the foothills close to the woods. The Count never issued restricted access there, and the grass is better than on the Commons."

"The woods are dangerous." Worry tinged Father's voice.

"I know." Gerd patted his shoulder. "But I'm always careful." He took the goat to its pen, washed his hands in the water basin beside the door, and returned to the table. "Wow, a cake." He hugged Frank. "What a surprise. How did you do that?"

Trying hard not to think how small the cake was for three people, Frank divided it and recounted how he'd made it. From the corner of his eye, he noticed his father standing beside the goat's pen, watching her. "The cake is ready. Are you coming?"

It seemed to him that his father left the pen rather reluctantly.

Time flew, and the cake shrank, then vanished into hungry mouths. It was good enough to make the taste of the acorn coffee bearable. They talked about what little news their small village had had in the past half year since the last merchant had visited. When the feast was over, Gerd was allowed to rest beside the fire while Frank washed the dishes. Irritated, he realized his father was already standing beside the goat's pen again. He walked over and reached out to put his hand on his father's arm.

"Did he feed you well?" Father's voice sounded pressed, as if something inside of him forced it past his lips. "Are you happy, dearest goat?"

"How can I be happy?" To Frank's great surprise, the goat answered. "After chasing me up the hill, Gerd forced me to jump over rivulets and walk in the shade of cursed trees. I didn't eat enough to feed a flea."

"Gerd!" Father shot around. Once more Frank noticed the reddish glow in his eyes. When his gaze traveled to the goat, looking miserable and forlorn, he found the same flicker in her eyes.

Father shot through the room like a steam car. He grabbed his son by the collar, pulled him off the stool, and shook him. "What have I taught you about lying to me?"

Frank's jaw dropped. Not once in his fifteen years of existence had he seen his father angry enough to turn violent.

"Get out of my house this very minute." Father opened the door and pushed Gerd through, despite how much his son protested. He dumped him in the mud outside, closed the door, and latched it. Then he walked to the stool by the fire and sat

"Let me in." Gerd banged against the door. "I didn't lie. I swear! Please, Father, let me in."

Father's shoulders slumped but he didn't move. Frank stood rooted to the spot, torn between opening the door again to let his brother in and fear of this unknown side of his father. Endless moments later, Gerd ceased his banging.

"Fine!" he shouted. "But don't think I'll ever come back, Father."

Frank could hear his footsteps squelch away. Finally he snapped out of his stupor. Hurriedly he grabbed whatever edibles he could find, which wasn't much, the threadbare blanket from Gerd's straw mattress and his spare pants. To his surprise, Father didn't try to stop him. He sat beside the fire like a man who'd lost a war. Frank tied everything into a bundle, unlatched the door, and ran after his brother, ignoring the rain.

Since there was only a single path Gerd could have taken, he caught up with him in no time. When he handed him the bundle, he wasn't entirely convinced that Gerd's cheeks were wet due to the rain only. He tried to comfort him.

"Something strange happened with Father. He acts as if he's under a spell." He hugged Gerd, and his brother clung to him as if *he* were the younger one.

"I'll never be able to come back." Gerd's voice was uncharacteristically low.

"That's not true." Frank tried his best to cheer him up despite the circumstances and the dismal weather. "The whole year, Father's been telling me how much he missed Otto. Try to find a job, and then come for a visit. I'm sure he'll be different then. I've never before seen him like that."

"You were visiting Gran the day Otto left. He acted just the same back then." Gerd let go and picked up the bundle he'd dropped, and turned to go. "I'll let you know where I end up. Thanks for the things."

Frank watched him walk toward the village until the night swallowed his silhouette, and the wetness on his face most certainly wasn't rainwater.

For several days, Frank eased into his new duties. It wasn't difficult to lead the goat to the pasture, but the pain in his chest was unbearable. He refused to talk more than absolutely necessary. When his sorrow abated, he made up his mind. It was time to learn more about what had happened, and since his father could barely remember the night, he decided to ask the goat.

Her white fur stood in nice contrast with the green pasture. Like Gerd, he preferred to take her to the meadows near the woods, where the Count didn't dare to claim ownership. When she'd eaten for a while, he pulled the big kitchen knife from his pocket and held it hidden beside him. He'd sharpened it the day before, and the blade sparkled in the sun, but she was on his other side and thus shouldn't be able to see it.

He waited under a tree until she walked close enough. Grabbing the goat's horns, he twisted her head, put the knife to her throat, and said, "I know you can talk. I heard you the day Father threw out Gerd. Why did you lie?"

The animal trembled and bleated, so he pressed the knife a little deeper into her soft fur.

"I'm not allowed to talk to you." The goat struggled to escape but Frank was strong. "Please let me go."

"Why did you lie to my father?"

"I had to. It's part of my curse." Frank withdrew the knife a little, and the goat continued. "My curse forces me to lie to all questions someone asks me on the evening of the sixteenth birthday of any young man that had herded me. It also forces the parents to hate their son and send them away. Most boys never return."

"Why don't you run away?" Frank let go of her horn. "You could live in the woods."

"I'm a goat." The animal sat on her haunches. "There are wolves and lynx in the woods. I wouldn't last a day."

"What are you going to do when I have been chased off too?" Frank sat in the grass and cocked his head, playing with his knife.

"I'll have to leave your father to find a new family with at least one son." The goat's head drooped, and Frank could make out a tear that seeped into the fur on her muzzle. "I hate, hate, hate my curse."

"Is there no way to break it?"

The goat shrugged, which looked decidedly weird with so much fur hanging from her shoulders.

"Let me get this straight," Frank said. "When I turn sixteen, your curse will force you to lie, and my father to chase me away like he did with Otto and Gerd, regardless how much he loves us?"

"Yes."

"And immediately after, you must run away to bring doom to another family?"

"Yes."

"So, we've obviously have very few options." Frank gazed at the knife in his hand. "We could turn you into a roast…"

"You wouldn't do that, would you?" The goat walked a few steps backward, the eyes in her furry face wide and her nostrils flaring.

"Only as a last resort." Frank grinned, showing his teeth. He knew that talking animals considered the display of teeth a threat. "But we've still got two more options. We could sell you."

"It's difficult." The goat didn't look as if she had calmed but she did her best to seem composed. "Only someone with sons will be able to buy me, and that way you'll probably not get the price you'd like to have."

"And it would leave us without a goat to milk, not speaking of the fact that we'd dump the problem onto someone else." Frank got up and put away the knife. "What would happen if I leave before my father can send me away?"

"I don't know if the curse would allow that. You're supposed to look after me. But no one ever tried, so I couldn't say."

"What if I take you along? Technically I'd still be looking after you, wouldn't I?" The more he thought about it, the more Frank liked his idea. The goat remained silent. He patted her. "We'll give it a try. Let's go home. I've got a lot to explain to Father."

"Are you sure you want to do that?" Father wrung his hands. Through the open door a chilly breeze announced the coming winter, but the sunlight was welcome. It saved them the need of burning a lamp. "You're my last son. What if you don't come back either?"

"I told you sending Otto and Gerd away wasn't your fault. Next spring you'd be forced to do the same to me." Frank stuffed his second pair of socks into his bundle. "I'll find my brothers and tell them all about this curse. I'm sure they'll come home with me."

"I'll miss you so much." Father put his arms around Frank, and they hugged. "Come back safely. How long do you think it'll take?"

"It depends on where they went. I might have to search for quite some time. But I will come back. I promise." Frank took the goat's leash he'd fashioned from string and walked through the door, followed by the animal and his father. He took the path downhill toward the village, waving back at every turn of the road until his home and his father were no longer visible.

In the village, a baker was able to tell him which road Gerd had traveled since he'd come up the same road in time for work that day. Frank thanked him and walked on. It took him three weeks to finally find his brother. Gerd was working in a mill and very happy to see him. When the miller heard who Frank was, he allowed them to sit on a bench outside and even provided them hot coffee.

"What a delight to have you here." Gerd hugged Frank. "I thought I'd never see you again in my life."

"Father sends his love." Frank noticed Gerd's frown and hastened to explain about the curse. He concluded his tale with, "Father begs you to come home. He's devastated about what the curse made him do."

"I'm so happy to hear that." Gerd smiled. "I will visit him as soon as I can, but I just started my apprenticeship with the miller. I only get a single day off once a month."

"Father is prepared to wait. Will you earn some money?" Frank asked.

"A little, why?"

"You could send him a letter. He's not as good at reading as we are but he'll manage if you write with big letters." Frank finished his coffee and got up. "Thank your miller for the drink."

"Do you have to go already?" Gerd's eyebrows rose. "I thought you'd stay at least for the night."

"I can't. I have to find Otto."

After much pleading from Gerd and the miller's wife, and because he knew he had brought fairly little to eat, Frank stayed for lunch. When he left, his bundle bulged with the food the miller's wife had forced on him, and he was certain that Gerd was going to be happy here.

He and the goat wandered around the kingdom looking for Otto until their food ran low again. Then Frank would work. He was lucky to look slightly older than he was, so most farmers didn't bother to ask for his papers. They were simply glad for the help. The year promised to yield a record harvest, which meant that every hand was needed. Frank talked to every person he met, but no one had seen Otto.

Then one day, a wheat merchant told him he'd seen a young man who fit the description working for a carpenter in the capital of the next kingdom. Frank set out immediately despite the goat's protest. The autumn winds and rains made traveling a chore. More often than not Frank huddled shivering against the goat in a forgotten barn or under a couple of bushes. His progress slowed, but he didn't give up. The day after the first night of snow he arrived at the gates of the neighboring kingdom's capital.

"Where to?" The guards stopped him with lowered lances. He didn't blame them. His clothes, well-worn when he set out, hung in tatters. Even the goat's fur was more gray than white.

"I'm looking for my brother." He told them about his travels and how hard it had been to come here.

"Vagabonds are prohibited in our city," one of the guards said. "And even if your tale is true, you look like one."

"But I have to talk to my brother." Frank's heart sank. He was considering kneeling and pleading when the second guard spoke.

"We understand your situation. Someone will accompany you to the carpenters' quarters to see if your brother truly is there." He waved to a third guard who stood beside a narrow door in the gatehouse. "But if your information is wrong and your brother is not in our city, you will leave before we close the doors for the night."

"Thank you, sir." Frank felt like kissing the guard's hands, but bowed instead. The third guard took him into town silently. Between the houses there was barely any wind. For the first time in a long while, Frank didn't shiver. The goat walked as close to him as possible. He thought it possible that she was as intimidated as he was by how many people there were in the streets. Open-mouthed he stared at the timber frame houses lining the narrow cobblestone streets, at the big windows of the houses' ground floors, displaying wares of every kind, and at the people hurrying to and fro. He'd never seen so many people in one place before.

"The quarter of the carpenters," the guard said. "What's your brother's name?"

Frank told him, and the man entered the first shop on the street. Frank stayed outside and admired wooden toys, picture frames, and furniture through the window. A few minutes later, the guard returned.

"It seems your information is correct." The guard set out at a brisk walk, and Frank hurried to follow him, the goat at his side. After a little while, when they had turned so many corners that Frank didn't know where they were, the guard pointed to a narrow but high house with a small shop window displaying wooden tables and chairs. "He should be working in there."

Frank entered the shop feeling out of place with his goat and the guard in tow. But he needn't have worried. The minute the carpenter learned who he was, he was pulled through a narrow passage connecting the shop with the workroom. Otto shed so many tears of joy that the sawdust the goat had claimed as her bed became wet. Satisfied, the guard left before the hugging came to an end.

"What a surprise to see you here." Otto didn't let go of Frank's hands. "I can't believe you traveled this far. It must have been a nightmare. Just look at you!"

"I'll tell the housekeeper to prepare a bath." The white-haired carpenter reached for the door to the house's living quarters. "And some new clothes and a little food for my best student's brother won't go amiss either, methinks."

Frank and his goat spent the whole winter with Otto and the carpenter. He did his best to convince his brother that their father deeply regretted what the curse had made him do, but Otto wouldn't relent.

"No curse in the world can make a father hate his own flesh and blood," he kept saying. And the goat wasn't much help either since she refused to talk to anyone but Frank.

With spring, Frank's sixteenth birthday approached. The morning before, he took the goat to the meadow beside the river outside the town where she had grazed every snow-free day that winter.

When she had eaten her fill, she said, "You know that you'll be chased away tomorrow, right?"

"Why's that? I thought only fathers are affected by the curse." Frank, lying on his back and cloud-gazing, yawned.

"Otto feels responsible for you, so it will affect him too." The goat cuddled up beside him. "I'll miss you."

Frank sat up with a jerk. "Why do we have to split up when I get chased away?"

"Because there's no brother left. I'll be forced to find a new family."

Frank's hands grew cold at the thought of losing the goat. "Is there no way around it?"

"One would need to break the spell's hold over me, but that'll never happen." The goat hung her head and sighed. They sat silently, pondering their quandary until night fell, and then Frank got up.

"I can't think of a way to break your spell," he said. "But I think I can make Otto understand what happened to Father."

Back in the carpenter's home, he found his brother in front of the kitchen fireplace cooking dinner.

Otto was ginning as if someone had given him the world. "Guess what? My master set up a new will, leaving the carpentry to me. He says I'm like the son he's never had."

"That's wonderful news," Frank said, but kept his features earnest. "I hope you'll be able to enjoy it when you chase me away tomorrow."

"I'll never do that. You can stay with me for however long you want." Otto laid aside the wooden spoon he was using to stir the stew and lifted a hand. "I swear."

The master carpenter came in to set the table. So far, Frank had ceased speaking of the curse whenever he showed up, but time was running out, and he needed to make Otto understand.

"The goat said that curse will force you, no matter how different you think about it today." He grabbed Otto's arm with both hands and looked him in the eyes. "You will chase me away, and that's a fact."

"I won't—" His brother tried to protest, but Frank didn't let him.

"Promise me one thing. One thing only." He stared into Otto's eyes until his brother nodded, then he continued. "I want you to reconsider your feelings for Father if you realize the day after tomorrow that you acted the same as he did."

"That'll never happen. You're my brother."

"Promise!"

"Fine, fine." Otto threw up his hands. "I promise that I'll visit Father should I sent you away on your birthday tomorrow."

The carpenter cleared his throat. "Why don't you break the curse?"

Surprised, Frank turned to the elderly man. "I've tried to find a way, but to no avail. I couldn't even think of a place where to start."

"There used to be an inventor in town who was well versed in all things magical." The carpenter filled the mugs with water. "If I remember correctly, he said that knowing a cursed one's name, or the true name of the witch or sorcerer, is half the bargain."

"I could question the goat. It's worth a try." Frank slipped into the seat beside him. "Where does this inventor live? Can I talk to him?"

"He moved to Bergia a long time ago." The carpenter smiled and waited until Otto had filled the plates with stew before he continued. "But Bergia is small and still quite steeped in magic, so you might be able to find him there. If Otto will really chase you away tomorrow, that's certainly a place to look."

Frank thanked the carpenter and decided to go to Bergia. As the subject of their discussion shifted, he dug into his stew.

The next day, when the goat had eaten enough and they were lying side by side in the grass near the river again, he asked for her name.

"My name is…" The last word sounded like a bleat.

"The person who cast the curse obviously didn't want anyone to know your name." Frank stared at her, his heart hammering in his chest. "It seems to be important. Maybe the carpenter is right. Try again."

The goat did, but no matter how often she repeated her name, it didn't become any clearer to Frank. "If only you could write." He sighed. "I bet the witch never thought about that."

"She probably didn't," the goat said. "But I was still a child when she changed me into a goat. I never learned to write. The only letter I know is the A."

"You were a human?" Frank's eyes widened. "I assumed you'd always been a talking goat."

"I was eight years old at that time." The goat's eyes filled with tears. "And it was my own mother who did this to me. I just hope she'll rot in hell for that."

"But why would a mother turn her own daughter into a goat?" Frank couldn't believe his ears. Unfortunately the goat's explanation was nothing but bleating. Another forbidden subject. Frank sighed. "We need to find out your name. Let's see if I can guess it. Is it Annabelle?"

"No."

"Anastasia?"

"No."

And so it went. Whatever name Frank came up with was rejected by the goat. When evening fell, he hit the ground with his fist out of frustration. Mud splattered his trousers.

"I've got an idea," the goat yelled. "Let's see if this works. Draw a bed in the mud."

Frank complied.

"And now draw a big A around it." The goat hopped excitedly around him. "Yes, like that. That's my name! I did it."

"Beda?" Frank's brow furrowed.

"No. Look closer. It's a riddle." The goat bounced around like a yeanling. "You need to spell out what you've got."

"A bed in an A." Frank's frown deepened. "Bed in A … Bedina … Bettina! Your name is Bettina?"

"Yes!" The goat bleated and bleated.

Frank thought he might have heard her repeating her name, so he said, "Please, Bettina, stay with me when Otto chases me away."

"My name is…" The goat bleated some more. After the third time, Frank was able to make out her name. "…Bettina, and I've got the feeling that I can stay with you. It seems that you did break part of the curse at least. Thank you so much."

The smile on Frank's face couldn't be wider as they walked back to the carpenter's home.

"Get out of the house this very minute." Otto opened the door and pushed Frank through no matter how much the carpenter protested. Frank barely managed to grab the bundle he'd prepared. At least this time he would go well-clad and with enough provisions for several days.

"Remember your promise," he said before turning and walking away. Bettina followed him even though he didn't use a leash any more. When they had left the city behind, Frank asked, "And what am I supposed to do now?"

"Find work," Bettina said. "I know that my mother will contact you sometime soon, she always does, so I'd better hide."

A longing pulled at Frank's heart at the thought of separating from her. "Promise to stay close."

"I will. After all, you've got to feed me and protect me from wild animals." For a second it seemed as if Bettina was smiling, then she bounced away and vanished in the ditch beside the road. Frank watched her until even the last trace of her white fur was gone, then he set out toward the woods.

He'd barely reached the edge when an old woman with a big bundle of twigs stepped from the trees' twilight. He greeted politely, and she put her bundle down and asked about his whereabouts.

"I'm looking for work, and since I'm young and healthy I'll surely find something," he said, noticing her calculating gaze. Could this be Bettina's mother?

"Why don't you become an apprentice?" the woman asked. "Sure, you'll earn less but you'll learn skills you'll always be able to use."

"I'm not suited for crafts like carpentry or milling." He tipped his head. "Thank you for the advice though."

"If you change your mind, there's a swordswoman in the next village looking for a trainee." The old woman picked up her bundle again and trundled toward the city.

When Frank walked under the trees, Bettina reappeared at his side. "That was my mother. In disguise, obviously, but her without a doubt."

"Why did she send me to a swordswoman?" Frank tried to find a good reason but came up blank. "Do I look like a fighter to you?"

"Yes." Bettina's bleating was definitely laughter.

Frank laughed with her. "Fine. I think to find out why your mother turned you into a goat and how to break the spell, I will probably have to do what she says. At least for a while."

They arrived at the next village when the sun was setting. On the way from the woods they passed an inn where Frank asked for the swordswoman. The innkeeper told him the way but his customers, a handful of farmers happy to be done for the day, laughed about him.

"A sparrow who wants to learn fighting from a swan," one called. "You might as well leave your balls here, lad."

Frank left the inn ignoring the laughter. A little later he knocked on the door of a small but well-kept timber frame house. A slender woman in tight-fitting black shirt and trousers with a wide, white overcoat opened with a frown on her beautiful face. Her gaze became hard when she saw Frank and Bettina.

"What do you want?"

Frank swallowed. The woman's muscles, emphasized by the black fabric of her dress, were impressive. He wouldn't want to get on the wrong side of her. "I'd like to become your apprentice if you don't mind."

"Of course. And my mother was the Empress of Eastland." The woman was about to close her door, but Frank put his foot in the gap even though he was convinced that the woman could smash it easily.

"I really want to learn your skills," he said, trying to sound as sincere as possible. "An old woman recommended you to me."

The woman hesitated. "What's the goat for then?"

"She keeps me company."

"People will laugh at you."

For a moment Frank thought she meant they'd laugh about his goat, but then he remembered the scene at the inn. "They already did. I don't care." Frank tried to look as determined as he imagined a wannabe apprentice should look. "If you're as good as the old woman said, you're the right teacher for me."

"I'll give you a two-week trial." The woman opened the door a little more. "Food and room included, one day off per month. The usual."

Frank nodded.

"You may address me as Master Sioban." The woman stepped aside and opened the door wide. Frank entered with Bettina at his heels.

During the next two weeks, Frank learned the basics of fighting and found that he enjoyed how his body began to shape up and his dexterity increased. He also liked his teacher's philosophy: never hit when talking is asked for, never maim if hitting will do, don't kill until absolutely necessary.

At the end of the trial, Master Sioban extended his apprenticeship for the full three years required to become a bodyguard. Bettina kept close to the house most of the time, but sometimes she went to check on his brothers. Life settled into a rhythm Frank liked. The only drawback was Bettina's growing sadness. On his free days, Frank went out to see if he could find Bettina's mother again. He wanted to interrogate her to see if she would tell him how to break the curse but he never found even a trace of her. Whenever he came back empty-handed, the goat looked a little more forlorn. It pulled on his heartstrings to see her so unhappy.

Time flew by.

A year after he began his training, Bettina left to check on Frank's brothers once more. When she returned, she was agitated. Frank noticed it even before she had entered the house.

"What's wrong?"

"Mother cheated your brother out of his well-earned payment." She pawed the ground as if she wanted to kick her mother.

"Start at the beginning. Which brother, what payment, and how was he cheated?" Frank stroked her back until she relaxed and told him the whole tale.

"Your brother Otto passed his exam as a carpenter, as the best trainee of his town. His master was so proud he gave him his most prized possession as payment: a magical table. With the right words it would set itself and provide you with a feast."

"Wow, that sounds like a cool gift." Frank put a bucket of fresh water down for the goat.

She drank a little and continued. "He's been full of remorse ever since he sent you away, so he decided that now was the time to visit your father. He took the table along to show him what he had achieved. When he arrived at your old home, your father was extremely happy to see him again, but the table was nothing but a table. Someone had swapped it for the magical table."

"How can you be so sure that it was your mother?"

"Because..." The rest of her words came out as bleating. Frustrated, she kicked the ground with her hind legs.

"Don't worry. I'll find out." Frank scratched his chin, pondering the seed of an idea. "Gerd will be done with his training sometime soon, too. Don't you think?"

The goat cocked her head. "I don't know. Why?"

"Let's visit him on my next free day." Frank smiled at Bettina. "I don't have a plan yet but if your mother really cheated Otto, and your bleating tells me there's a reason for that, it seems reasonable to assume that she's done the same with all the boys your curse forced away from home."

"So?" Bettina's brow wrinkled. "I don't see your point."

"She'll try Gerd next."

It turned out that Gerd's final exams were still half a year off, but he promised to send word when he finished. Frank returned to his usual routine. The training and meditation seemed to sharpen his senses which he enjoyed very much. Only his reading, writing, and calculating lessons were unloved, although he admitted that all were useful skills. Despite his dislike, he put his best effort into all the subjects Master Sioban decided to teach him, and she was pleased with his progress.

One evening in autumn, a messenger brought a spoken note from Gerd. "Your brother sends you these words: I finished my training well. My master was so pleased by my good grades that he granted me my greatest wish. He allowed me to wed his daughter whom I love very much. The day after tomorrow I'll set out on his donkey to fetch Father for the wedding."

"I'm assuming you'd want an extra day off for the wedding," Master Sioban said after the messenger had left. She pulled a face which made it perfectly clear that she didn't like the interruption of their schedule.

"No, Master." Frank bowed. "But I would like to ask permission to take my free day tomorrow instead of next week."

Master Sioban pulled up an eyebrow. Frank knew she needed a reason for his strange request, but could he tell her about the curse? What if she decided to get rid of Bettina? On the other hand, he'd gotten to know her as a sensible woman who wasn't afraid of anything, not even magic. After some pondering, he decided to tell her all. He started with the day he had found out about the curse, and ended with his reasoning for the day off.

"The messenger has been traveling for a full day, so Gerd will leave the mill tomorrow morning. If I leave here at the same time, I can intercept him on the way to my father. I might find the witch that way."

Master Sioban pouted, then said, "Fighting a witch is very dangerous. You haven't had the right training yet, and I can't accompany you because of an important guild meeting I have to attend tomorrow." She sighed. "Promise me that you will not try to fight her."

"I have to talk to her to find out how to save Bettina." Frank stood straight. He knew he had no chance against his master should she decide to settle their disagreement with a fight, but he was prepared to defend himself as best he could.

"And I will give you the means to do just that," Master Sioban said. "But for my little trick to work, you'll need to get very close to the witch, which you cannot do if she turns you into a frog."

"I'm fast. I can escape her spells, I'm sure." Frank wasn't ready to give up on his plan, although he had to admit that it was a half-baked one.

"She'd still recognize you when you return." Master Sioban put her hand on his arm. "Stay hidden and observe her. Find out where she meets the cursed boys and how she swindles them out of their hard-earned gains, and see where she goes after the deed if you can."

Frank pressed his lips together.

The woman smiled. "And then, we'll set up a trap for her." She began to explain.

Frank relaxed. Her idea sounded like a much better plan than his. When he nodded eagerly to every word she said, she grinned.

"I think I'll put strategy on your schedule early. Setting up the right surprise for your enemy truly is the most important part of winning a fight."

Frank and Bettina set out before dawn. Bettina carried a sack with provisions Master Sioban had given them. They made good progress and reached the road that led from the mill to the village where Frank's father lived in the late afternoon. Frank examined the ground. Last night's rain had erased all tracks older than today's.

"He hasn't come through yet," he said. "Only someone with an ox-cart, a horse rider, and a couple of people on foot."

"Good," Bettina said. "I'm hungry." Since she was still a goat, she found some grass and began to nibble. Frank untied the provisions and dug in too. He'd just finished his meal when Gerd walked out of the village a little farther down the road leading a donkey. Frank waved, and Gerd waved back. When they met, they hugged and shared their most important news before traveling on.

"You won't make it to Father today," Frank said. "Not even riding a donkey."

"Oh, Toddler here isn't for riding." Gerd beamed. "If I use the correct phrase, he shits gold. See?" He opened a purse on his belt and let Frank see inside. It was filled with golden coins. "My master gave him to me in case I run into an emergency. He and his daughter want me back as soon as possible."

"Which is totally understandable." Frank watched the donkey, scratching his chin. "So you've got a magical item too. I'm sensing a pattern here." He turned to the goat. "Bettina, did all the boys that were affected by the curse end up with something magical?"

The goat bleated and nodded at the same time.

"I see." Frank was proud that he'd discovered another piece of the puzzle, especially since it fitted in extremely well with his master's plan. He turned back to Gerd. "Where do you intend to spend the night?"

"There's an inn halfway up the mountain." Gerd pointed to a house well ahead of them.

"Okay. Here's the deal." Frank bent closer to his brother. "You know that I'm training as a bodyguard. I'm on a secret mission, investigating something my master needs to know. Swear that you won't tell anyone that you met me."

"Oh, you're taking your final exam so soon?" Gerd's eyes widened.

"Not by a long shot." Frank smiled. "But it's an important part of my education, so I can't bungle it. It's just that I really wanted to see you again."

"That's no problem. I'll erase you from my memory." He hugged Frank, but his voice sounded amused as he said, "I wish you a lot of success on your secret mission."

Frank remained beside a group of bushes and watched Gerd until his brother tied the donkey to a ring in the inn's wall and went inside.

"You'd better stay here, Bettina," Frank said. When she nodded, he made his way to the back of the inn's stable using every cover he could find. He was just about to dart to one of the inn's windows when the innkeeper and Gerd came out again.

"He'll be perfectly happy in the stable," the innkeeper said. "I've got the best oats."

Frank ducked and hid behind a water barrel while Gerd untied his donkey and led it into the stable. Only when the two men had returned to the warmth of the inn's taproom did he dare to come out of hiding again. For a moment he hesitated but it seemed easier to keep an eye on the donkey than on the innkeeper and any staff, should there be some. He entered the stable through the backdoor. When his eyes had adjusted to the din interior, he made out two pens with donkeys, one with a horse, and an oversized pen with chickens. Beside the horse's pen, a ladder led to a storage area filled with straw and sacks of grain. He climbed up, found himself a hiding place in the straw above the pens and waited.

Time dragged, and he struggled with boredom. Very, very slowly the light dimmed and the world grew quiet. Through a window in the stable's gable he saw the lights in the inn go out one after the other. His eyelids drooped, but he managed to stay awake. He was just thinking about climbing back down to the ground to wet his face with water from the barrel and refresh himself, when the stable door opened. The innkeeper came in, carrying a lantern. Immediately Frank was wide awake.

"Well, well," the innkeeper said when he looked into the donkey's pen. "You're quite the beauty. Now, let's see if your owner told me the right word. Bricklebrit."

The donkey hee-hawed three times, and in the following silence, Frank heard the ring of coins dropping on coins.

"Well done, little donkey," the innkeeper said. He pointed a finger at the animal and said a strange word that rang in Frank's ears like the reverberation of a church bell. He winced. When he looked again, there was a mouse in place of the donkey. The innkeeper put it into a small wooden box he carried in a pouch on his belt. Then he pointed at the second donkey and said another word that also reverberated through Frank's head. The donkey changed color until it looked exactly like the one Gerd had brought. Frank balled his hands to fists. How he longed to punish the thieving innkeeper. Could he be Bettina's mother? Frank wasn't sure. The figure below him looked as male as any potbellied man he had ever seen. Grinding his teeth, he tried hard to keep his anger under control. Only the promise he'd made to his master kept him from jumping the scumbag. His involuntary movements made the straw he was hiding in crackle.

"Who's there?" The innkeeper shot around, lifting his lantern.

Frank held his breath. The innkeeper took a few steps toward the ladder when a small figure stepped out of the shadows.

"Hello, mother," Bettina said. So the innkeeper was Bettina's mother in disguise, just like Frank had suspected.

"Why aren't you working on your next job?" The disguised witch lifted her lamp some more, scanned the straw, luckily without noticing Frank, and then focused on the goat.

"I took a night off." Bettina stepped closer. "You promised me you'd tell me how to break this spell. Remember?"

"I just said that to get you out of the house. It's unbreakable." The witch laughed. "But it'll dissolve on its own when my needs are fulfilled."

Bettina said something, but to Frank it sounded like beating.

The witch obviously understood because she answered. "I decide when I have enough, and it's none of your business where I take them. They're mine."

"One day, someone will find out what you're doing, and then you'll get burnt at the stake." Bettina's voice sounded worried. Did she still love her mother despite what she had done to her?

"That'll never happen. Now, away with you, back to your job." The witch waved her hand, and a strong wind blew against Bettina. The more the goat struggled, the harder the wind blew. Eventually it pushed her out of the backdoor. As soon as she was gone, the disguised witch picked up the gold coins and left too. Frank waited until he was sure she wouldn't return, and then left through the backdoor to find Bettina.

She was waiting for him under a cluster of trees a little down the road.

"That confirms what I suspected," he said to her.

"What are you going to do?" Despite her goat face, Bettina looked worried. "I mean, she still is my mother."

"We'll talk to my master," Frank said and began his march back.

Close to sunset nearly two days later they stood under the very same trees with Master Sioban and watched the innkeeper put the shutters up for the night.

"And you're absolutely sure it's the witch?" Master Sioban asked.

Frank nodded, then pointed to two travelers with a donkey coming down the hill. "Look, I think those are my father and brother. It seems they'll spend the night there."

"Training then." Master Sioban smiled. "We'll listen without them noticing. Let me see how silent you can be."

Leaving Bettina behind, they slipped closer and closer to the inn. From tree to bush, from bush to barrel, from barrel to a corner of the house, and from there to a low bench below the window of the taproom. There they sat in silence and listened to the discussion inside.

83

"I know it was you. I never took my eyes off the donkey anywhere else," Gerd said.

"But I told you. I have not been here the last two days. I always take a little holiday once a year. I was with my sister in town." The unfamiliar, high and imploring voice must be that of the innkeeper.

"Where…" The sound of a slap rang out and the innkeeper whined.

"Is…" Another slap, another whimper.

"My…" Slap, cry.

"Donkey?" A loud crash made the shutters rattle. Something heavy must have bumped against the wall inside the house.

"Come, Gerd." Their father's voice was calm. "It's no use. It's your word against his. You'll never see your donkey again."

"My father-in-law will kill me." Gerd sounded very worried. "What if he cancels my wedding? If I can't even take care of a donkey, how can I protect my beloved?"

"You wouldn't leave your wife in a stable, now would you?" The voices dimmed as the two men walked up the stairs to their sleeping chambers.

"That sounds as if your witch impersonated the innkeeper," Master Sioban said. "Let me check if that's right." She slipped out of the house's shadow, walked to the front door and entered. Frank pulled up his hood and followed her into the taproom. He found her bent over the innkeeper with a knife at his throat.

"...not here, I swear." Tears were running over the innkeeper's fat cheeks. "Once a year I get the urge to travel. It annoys my sister no end, but she can attest that I've been with her."

"Who is running your inn when you're gone?" Master Sioban's voice was barely more than a hiss.

"No one. Really. I close the inn and hide the key." He sobbed. "Please. I didn't do anything. Don't kill me."

Frank smelled the sharp odor of urine and felt sorry for the man. As abruptly as she had come, his master turned and left, grabbing his arm and pulling him along. When they reached the cluster of trees again, she sat down and said, "It seems that the witch has a way to know when one of the boys the curse drove out of their homes is traveling. She puts a compulsion on the innkeeper who can't help but visit his sister and takes his place. As long as we don't know where she's hiding the rest of the time, we can't do anything right now. If you can't find her, you'll have to wait until you pass your exam."

"It's got nothing to do with the exams," Bettina said. "It's because of..." The rest of her sentence sounded like the bleating of a real goat once more. Frank was so fed up he could have screamed.

"Does it have something to do with the reason why they're traveling?" Master Sioban asked.

Bettina shook her head.

Frank had an inspiration. "Does it have to do with something they're bringing along?"

Bettina nodded.

"Something they didn't have before?"

Bettina nodded again.

"Something like Gerd's donkey and Otto's table?"

Bettina bleated and nodded at the same time.

"She's stealing magical objects!" Frank slapped his forehead. "She cursed her own daughter only to gain some magical gadgets. How crazy is that?"

Master Sioban bent forward and looked Bettina in the eyes. "Does she know which magical item is coming her way?"

Bettina shook her head. She seemed very satisfied. "Finally I can tell you all. Magic has some strange rules. Mother can feel if a craftsman owns something worth stealing, but she can't take it from him directly. But she can compel him to take on a student and request whatever she wants as payment for sending him a suitable subject although he didn't know about her."

Master Sioban chuckled. "If that's true, I've got just the thing for her. Frank, tell your brother to leave the fake donkey here. He's to tell his father-in-law that you'll be bringing the animal to the wedding. When was it again?"

"In three days," Frank said, feeling a little bewildered.

"That's plenty of time." Master Sioban stood straight and stretched. "Come home as soon as you talked to your brother. I'll teach you how to defeat a witch."

Two days later, Frank hid in the cluster of trees near the inn with a sack holding a cudgel beside him and admitted to himself that his master's plan seemed to be working. The innkeeper left the house around noon with a knapsack over his shoulder and walked downhill at a swift pace but with a vacant stare. When he turned a corner, the very same innkeeper left the house and checked the stable before returning to the house. *Fine,* Frank thought. *The witch is in.* He patted Bettina.

"Stay here. If anything goes wrong, fetch Master Sioban."

He picked up the sack with the cudgel, backtracked his path, circled the hill and walked up the road as if he'd come from the city. Even though he tried, he couldn't see Bettina. *Brave girl.*

He strode right into the inn's taproom, ordered a milk, and sat at a table near one of the windows, patting his sack several times.

"No beer for the young man?" The witch in her innkeeper disguise pointed to the keg behind the counter.

"No thanks. I've still got a way to travel today." Frank declined. "I just need a short rest."

"Some food then?" The witch-innkeeper rubbed his hands on a towel. "We've got mutton stew today."

"Sounds good." Frank opened the sack, looked inside, and closed it again. "Can I get a copper's worth?"

"Coming up." The witch left through a door behind the counter. She returned with a steaming bowl and a mug a few minutes later and set both on the table near the window in front of Frank. Her eyes clung to the sack. "A mighty fine sack you've got there."

"My master gave it to me." Frank made sure to stick to the truth. Master Sioban had told him that most witches could sense lies. "It's magical."

"What does it do?" The witch's eyes were wide and filled with greed.

"Can't tell you. It's a secret." Frank smiled, trying to make it look apologetic instead of smug. *Hook, line and sinker.*

"I'm not one to pry." The witch nodded to him and pointed to the stew. "It's best hot. I hope you'll like it."

"Smells delicious." He dipped the spoon in the bowl and hesitated. "May I open the window? It's rather warm in here."

"Sure, go ahead." The witch began to wipe tables near him while Frank opened a window. Then he lifted a spoonful of stew to his lips and blew on it. Loud bleating sounded from outdoors, and he had to hide his smile. Bettina's timing couldn't be better.

The witch's head spun around and she frowned. Hurriedly, she walked to the front door and looked out, but Frank knew she wouldn't see his friend. He used the time the witch was gone and emptied half the bowl and the mug out of the window. Just as the witch returned he put the mug to his mouth pretending he'd drunk. He noticed the satisfied flicker in her eyes.

"Shall I refill the mug?" She held out her hand.

"That'd be," he yawned, "nice."

When she returned, he had slumped in his seat and pretended to be asleep. With a gleeful cackle, the witch set the mug aside and grabbed the sack.

"An idiot like all the others." She opened the sack's strings and looked inside. A frown appeared on her face. "What's it for? How do you activate it?"

Frank felt the magical command like a cuff to his stomach. It was hard to only answer one of the questions but he managed. Loud and commanding he said, "Cudgel, out!"

Immediately the cudgel jumped out of the sack and began to dance on the witch's back. She dropped the sack and tried to evade the blows, screaming and shouting the whole time. It was a merry dance, and the cudgel led. If it dipped right, the witch turned left and vice versa.

Frank sat up and laughed with delight. "Didn't expect that, did you?"

"Please, lad," she screamed. "I'll do anything you want. Just tell it to stop."

"Where are the magical gadgets your stole?" Frank bent forward.

"Tell it to stop and I'll show you." The witch danced around a chair with the cudgel slapping her hip, her bottom, her shoulder and every other exposed part.

"Show me and I might tell it to stop." This time, Frank allowed the smugness to show in his smile. Unlike the witch, he knew that the cudgel would not beat her to pulp. He'd not used the command for that. The beating would only be a hard lesson on what he thought of thieving.

"They're here." The witch transformed instantly into a middle-aged woman in a brown linen dress with a white apron and waved a bracelet at him. Due to the speed of her change, Frank realized her innkeeper disguise must have been an illusion rather than a real transformation.

"Hand them over." He held out his hand. Still trying to evade the cudgel, the witch fumbled with the bracelet's clasp. When she finally got it open, she hurled the bracelet to Frank. He examined it closely. It seemed to be made of silver and lots of miniature charms hung from it. There was a tiny table, a fiddle, a donkey, a goose, a spindle, a cup and many more. None of the items was bigger than the nail on his thumb. He unfastened them and laid them out side by side in the taproom while the cudgel hovered over the witch, who was trying to hide under a table in a corner. She was covering her head with both arms and whimpering the whole time. The hair escaping from her bun made her look like a straw-stuffed scarecrow.

"Return them to the way they were," Frank ordered, "or the cudgel will start slapping you around some more."

The witch pointed a finger at the silver trinkets and said a string of words that didn't make sense to Frank, although he could feel an icy draft coming from the witch's direction. Immediately the small items began to grow.

"Can I come out now?" The witch's voice sounded pleading, but held an aggressive undertone.

Still, Frank nodded. "If you don't try anything stupid."

She crawled out of her hiding place and moved to a wall close to the exit. Frank walked over to her and stood beside her with the cudgel hovering close. The bigger the magical objects grew, the more crowded the room became.

"Now, tell me how to break the spell you cast on your own daughter, and you'll be free to go." Frank looked directly into the witch's eyes. If gazes could kill, he would have dropped dead that instant.

"Rot in hell." The witch spat in his face.

It cost Frank a lot not to explode, but he managed to keep his temper. He wiped his face with his handkerchief and said, "You're obviously still misinterpreting the situation. I will not allow you to return to your thieving ways, and I will not let you have Bettina back."

The witch's face paled when he said her daughter's name, but she pressed her lips together and remained silent.

Frank nodded to the cudgel. "Twist and sing," he ordered.

The cudgel began to turn. A low whine grew in intensity the faster it spun. Frank had to put his fingers into his ears, but the witch seemed rooted to the spot, with her hands held in front of her face, palms outward in a gesture of self-defense. Thin, grayish threads flowed from her fingertips and the cudgel caught them and wound them around itself like a spindle. It stopped when no more threads flowed from the witch. When it began to absorb the grayish material, the witch screamed and flew at Frank.

"I'll kill you!" Her fingernails came dangerously close to his eyes, but he'd been expecting an attack, so he evaded her at the last possible moment, enjoying the way his body reacted. He let her rant and used her angry charging to test some of the moves his teacher had drilled into him. Naturally it wasn't easy to maneuver through the pile of items and animals that filled the taproom. When the witch ran out of steam, he grabbed her by the collar and dragged her to the door.

"Time for you to leave," he said.

"Give me back my magic." She was crying but no longer had the strength to struggle.

"Not a chance." Frank let go of her and she sank to the floor right in front of the inn.

"Get up and leave." Bettina stepped around the house's corner, lowered her head and trotted toward her. "Go and find yourself a place where you can earn money like an honest citizen. Maybe I'll forgive you in a few years."

Frank's heart sank. He'd so hoped that Bettina would regain her true form when the witch's magic was gone. No such luck though. Silently the two of them watched the witch slink away. The woman couldn't stop crying but they remained unmoved. She had caused too much pain to too many families. When she was no longer visible, Frank and Bettina went back inside and looked at the curious mix in the taproom. Everything had resumed its natural state by now, and the animals made a racket that made it hard to speak.

"I think it'll take us quite a while to find out what belongs to whom," Frank shouted over the din.

"Master Sioban is waiting in the woods with a horse-drawn cart." Bettina leaned against him, and he scratched her back absentmindedly. She leaned into him. "We should be able to get it all packed and loaded, so we can be at your brother's wedding with the donkey in time."

Frank looked down at his companion and a wave of empathy filled his heart. Even knowing that there might not be a cure for her curse, she still stood by him, helped him and never complained about her life. On an impulse, he bent down and kissed her wet nose.

Her form shimmered and flowed, moving and twisting as if no longer fixed in the shape he knew. It grew taller and gained human shape before it solidified again. In front of Frank stood a girl his age with long brown hair and wide, doe-like eyes. Very slowly a smile spread over her features.

"You did it." Her voice was barely more than a whisper. Frank was just about to take her into his arms for a real embrace and a better kiss, when she got pushed aside.

Master Sioban entered and looked around. "Wow! What a mess," she said. "Let's get this sorted right now. We wouldn't want the magical objects to have strange interactions."

Laughing, Bettina set to work, soon followed by Frank.

"At least," he said when they had loaded everything that wasn't alive onto Master Sioban's cart, "life will never be boring as long as we've got stolen goods to return to their rightful owners."

"You opted for an exciting life the moment you decided not to leave Bettina to her fate." Master Sioban patted his shoulder and laughed. Then she led the pony along the road toward her home. The cart rumbled along. Except for the donkey, all the animals were either tied to it or stored somewhere inside. She called over her shoulder, "As to how exciting it's going to be, you'll find out when you have children."

But Bettina and Frank were too busy kissing to hear her words.

THE ORIGINAL: CINDERELLA
by the Brothers Grimm

A rich man's wife became sick, and when she felt that her end was drawing near, she called her only daughter to her bedside and said, "Dear child, remain pious and good, and then our dear God will always protect you, and I will look down on you from heaven and be near you." With this she closed her eyes and died.

The girl went out to her mother's grave every day and wept, and she remained pious and good. When winter came the snow spread a white cloth over the grave, and when the spring sun had removed it again, the man took himself another wife.

This wife brought two daughters into the house with her. They were beautiful, with fair faces, but evil and dark hearts. Times soon grew very bad for the poor stepchild.

"Why should that stupid goose sit in the parlor with us?" they said. "If she wants to eat bread, then she will have to earn it. Out with this kitchen maid!"

They took her beautiful clothes away from her, dressed her in an old gray smock, and gave her wooden shoes. "Just look at the proud princess! How decked out she is!" they shouted and laughed as they led her into the kitchen.

There she had to do hard work from morning until evening, get up before daybreak, carry water, make the fires, cook, and wash. Besides this, the sisters did everything imaginable to hurt her. They made fun of her, scattered peas and lentils into the ashes for her, so that she had to sit and pick them out again. In the evening when she had worked herself weary, there was no bed for her. Instead she had to sleep by the hearth in the ashes. And because she always looked dusty and dirty, they called her Cinderella.

One day it happened that the father was going to the fair, and he asked his two stepdaughters what he should bring back for them.

"Beautiful dresses," said the one.

"Pearls and jewels," said the other.

"And you, Cinderella," he said, "what do you want?"

"Father, break off for me the first twig that brushes against your hat on your way home."

So he bought beautiful dresses, pearls, and jewels for his two stepdaughters. On his way home, as he was riding through a green thicket, a hazel twig brushed against him and knocked off his hat. Then he broke off the twig and took it with him. Arriving home, he gave his stepdaughters the things that they had asked for, and he gave Cinderella the twig from the hazel bush.

Cinderella thanked him, went to her mother's grave, and planted the branch on it, and she wept so much that her tears fell upon it and watered it. It grew and became a beautiful tree.

Cinderella went to this tree three times every day, and beneath it she wept and prayed. A white bird came to the tree every time, and whenever she expressed a wish, the bird would throw down to her what she had wished for.

Now it happened that the king proclaimed a festival that was to last three days. All the beautiful young girls in the land were invited, so that his son could select a bride for himself. When the two stepsisters heard that they too had been invited, they were in high spirits.

They called Cinderella, saying, "Comb our hair for us. Brush our shoes and fasten our buckles. We are going to the festival at the king's castle."

Cinderella obeyed, but wept, because she too would have liked to go to the dance with them. She begged her stepmother to allow her to go.

"You, Cinderella?" she said. "You, all covered with dust and dirt, and you want to go to the festival?. You have neither clothes nor shoes, and yet you want to dance!"

However, because Cinderella kept asking, the stepmother finally said, "I have scattered a bowl of lentils into the ashes for you. If you can pick them out again in two hours, then you may go with us."

The girl went through the back door into the garden, and called out, "You tame pigeons, you turtledoves, and all you birds beneath the sky, come and help me to gather:

The good ones go into the pot,

The bad ones go into your crop."

Two white pigeons came in through the kitchen window, and then the turtledoves, and finally all the birds beneath the sky came whirring and swarming in, and lit around the ashes. The pigeons nodded their heads and began to pick, pick, pick, pick. And the others also began to pick, pick, pick, pick. They gathered all the good grains into the bowl. Hardly one hour had passed before they were finished, and they all flew out again.

The girl took the bowl to her stepmother, and was happy, thinking that now she would be allowed to go to the festival with them.

But the stepmother said, "No, Cinderella, you have no clothes, and you don't know how to dance. Everyone would only laugh at you."

Cinderella began to cry, and then the stepmother said, "You may go if you are able to pick two bowls of lentils out of the ashes for me in one hour," thinking to herself, "She will never be able to do that."

The girl went through the back door into the garden, and called out, "You tame pigeons, you turtledoves, and all you birds beneath the sky, come and help me to gather:

The good ones go into the pot,

The bad ones go into your crop."

Two white pigeons came in through the kitchen window, and then the turtledoves, and finally all the birds beneath the sky came whirring and swarming in, and lit around the ashes. The pigeons nodded their heads and began to pick, pick, pick, pick. And the others also began to pick, pick, pick, pick. They gathered all the good grains into the bowls. Before a half hour had passed they were finished, and they all flew out again.

The girl took the bowls to her stepmother, and was happy, thinking that now she would be allowed to go to the festival with them.

But the stepmother said, "It's no use. You are not coming with us, for you have no clothes, and you don't know how to dance. We would be ashamed of you." With this she turned her back on Cinderella, and hurried away with her two proud daughters.

Now that no one else was at home, Cinderella went to her mother's grave beneath the hazel tree, and cried out:

Shake and quiver, little tree,

Throw gold and silver down to me.

Then the bird threw a gold and silver dress down to her, and slippers embroidered with silk and silver. She quickly put on the dress and went to the festival.

Her stepsisters and her stepmother did not recognize her. They thought she must be a foreign princess, for she looked so beautiful in the golden dress. They never once thought it was Cinderella, for they thought that she was sitting at home in the dirt, looking for lentils in the ashes.

The prince approached her, took her by the hand, and danced with her. Furthermore, he would dance with no one else. He never let go of her hand, and whenever anyone else came and asked her to dance, he would say, "She is my dance partner."

She danced until evening, and then she wanted to go home. But the prince said, "I will go along and escort you," for he wanted to see to whom the beautiful girl belonged. However, she eluded him and jumped into the pigeon coop. The prince waited until her father came, and then he told him that the unknown girl had jumped into the pigeon coop.

The old man thought, "Could it be Cinderella?"

He had them bring him an ax and a pick so that he could break the pigeon coop apart, but no one was inside. When they got home Cinderella was lying in the ashes, dressed in her dirty clothes. A dim little oil-lamp was burning in the fireplace. Cinderella had quickly jumped down from the back of the pigeon coop and had run to the hazel tree. There she had taken off her beautiful clothes and laid them on the grave, and the bird had taken them away again. Then, dressed in her gray smock, she had returned to the ashes in the kitchen.

The next day when the festival began anew, and her parents and her stepsisters had gone again, Cinderella went to the hazel tree and said:

Shake and quiver, little tree,

Throw gold and silver down to me.

Then the bird threw down an even more magnificent dress than on the preceding day. When Cinderella appeared at the festival in this dress, everyone was astonished at her beauty. The prince had waited until she came, then immediately took her by the hand, and danced only with her. When others came and asked her to dance with them, he said, "She is my dance partner."

When evening came she wanted to leave, and the prince followed her, wanting to see into which house she went. But she ran away from him and into the garden behind the house. A beautiful tall tree stood there, on which hung the most magnificent pears. She climbed as nimbly as a squirrel into the branches, and the prince did not know where she had gone. He waited until her father came, then said to him, "The unknown girl has eluded me, and I believe she has climbed up the pear tree.

The father thought, "Could it be Cinderella?" He had an ax brought to him and cut down the tree, but no one was in it. When they came to the kitchen,

Cinderella was lying there in the ashes as usual, for she had jumped down from the other side of the tree, had taken the beautiful dress back to the bird in the hazel tree, and had put on her gray smock.

On the third day, when her parents and sisters had gone away, Cinderella went again to her mother's grave and said to the tree:

Shake and quiver, little tree,
Throw gold and silver down to me.

This time the bird threw down to her a dress that was more splendid and magnificent than any she had yet had, and the slippers were of pure gold. When she arrived at the festival in this dress, everyone was so astonished that they did not know what to say. The prince danced only with her, and whenever anyone else asked her to dance, he would say, "She is my dance partner."

When evening came Cinderella wanted to leave, and the prince tried to escort her, but she ran away from him so quickly that he could not follow her. The prince, however, had set a trap. He had had the entire stairway smeared with pitch. When she ran down the stairs, her left slipper stuck in the pitch. The prince picked it up. It was small and dainty, and of pure gold.

The next morning, he went with it to the man, and said to him, "No one shall be my wife except for the one whose foot fits this golden shoe."

The two sisters were happy to hear this, for they had pretty feet. With her mother standing by, the older one took the shoe into her bedroom to try it on. She could not get her big toe into it, for the shoe was too small for her. Then her mother gave her a knife and said, "Cut off your toe. When you are queen you will no longer have to go on foot."

The girl cut off her toe, forced her foot into the shoe, swallowed the pain, and went out to the prince. He took her on his horse as his bride and rode away with her. However, they had to ride past the grave, and there, on the hazel tree, sat the two pigeons, crying out:

Rook di goo, rook di goo!

There's blood in the shoe.

The shoe is too tight,

This bride is not right!

Then he looked at her foot and saw how the blood was running from it. He turned his horse around and took the false bride home again, saying that she was not the right one, and that the other sister should try on the shoe. She went into her bedroom, and got her toes into the shoe all right, but her heel was too large.

Then her mother gave her a knife, and said, "Cut a piece off your heel. When you are queen you will no longer have to go on foot."

The girl cut a piece off her heel, forced her foot into the shoe, swallowed the pain, and went out to the prince. He took her on his horse as his bride and rode away with her. When they passed the hazel tree, the two pigeons were sitting in it, and they cried out:

Rook di goo, rook di goo!

There's blood in the shoe.
The shoe is too tight,
This bride is not right!

He looked down at her foot and saw how the blood was running out of her shoe, and how it had stained her white stocking all red. Then he turned his horse around and took the false bride home again.

"This is not the right one, either," he said. "Don't you have another daughter?"

"No," said the man. "There is only a deformed little Cinderella from my first wife, but she cannot possibly be the bride."

The prince told him to send her to him, but the mother answered, "Oh, no, she is much too dirty. She cannot be seen."

But the prince insisted on it, and they had to call Cinderella. She first washed her hands and face clean, and then went and bowed down before the prince, who gave her the golden shoe. She sat down on a stool, pulled her foot out of the heavy wooden shoe, and put it into the slipper, and it fitted her perfectly.

When she stood up the prince looked into her face, and he recognized the beautiful girl who had danced with him. He cried out, "She is my true bride."

The stepmother and the two sisters were horrified and turned pale with anger. The prince, however, took Cinderella onto his horse and rode away with her. As they passed by the hazel tree, the two white pigeons cried out:

Rook di goo, rook di goo!
No blood's in the shoe.
The shoe's not too tight,
This bride is right!

After they had cried this out, they both flew down and lit on Cinderella's shoulders, one on the right, the other on the left, and remained sitting there.

When the wedding with the prince was to be held, the two false sisters came, wanting to gain favor with Cinderella and to share her good fortune. When the bridal couple walked into the church, the older sister walked on their right side and the younger on their left side, and the pigeons pecked out one eye from each of them. Afterwards, as they came out of the church, the older one was on the left side, and the younger one on the right side, and then the pigeons pecked out the other eye from each of them. And thus, for their wickedness and falsehood, they were punished with blindness as long as they lived.

THE DWARF AND THE TWINS
SNOW WHITE AND ROSE RED
Treasures Retold 1

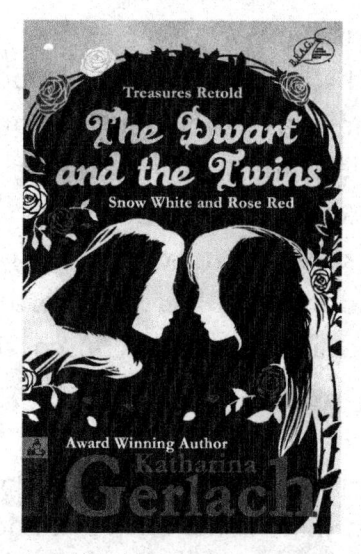

Once upon a time in a world where magic and technology collide with unexpected consequences…

When Martin helps a pregnant woman to flee from the king's men, he doesn't know that the twins she bears will change his solitary life forever.

What if the Brother's Grimm misunderstood the dwarf in the original tale of "Snow White and Rose Red"?

The book includes a bonus story and the original fairy tale.

ISBN 978-3-95681-028-2
auch als eBook erhältlich

Leave your eMail address so I can inform you about new releases, and this book will arrive as an eBook in your Inbox shortly after

http://www.katharinagerlach.com/readers

THE INHERITANCE
PUSS IN BOOTS
Treasures Retold 10

Once upon a time in a world where magic and technology collide with unexpected consequences…

The cat is caught in a curse with no way out. Not even the death of his hot-tempered owner, the miller, opens an escape route. Instead the youngest of the miller's sons inherits him. Can the cat gain his freedom if he fulfills the boy's impossible wish??

What if the Brother's Grimm hadn't known who or what „Puss in Boots" really is?

The book includes a bonus story and the original fairy tale.

available in winter 2017

CPSIA information can be obtained
at www.ICGtesting.com
Printed in the USA
FSOW03n1503191217
42572FS